Other Books by Bob Mustin

A Reason to Tremble
A Place of Belonging
The Blue Bicycle
Sam's Place - Stories
We Are Strong But We Are Fragile
Collateral Damage and Stories
In This Love Together - A Memoir
The Third Reich's Last Eagle
Gerbert's Book

A House
in the
Neighborhood

By

Bob Mustin

GRIDLEY FIRES

First Published by Gridley Fires Books, 7/01/2021

Gridley Fires Books and its logo are trademarked
by
Gridley Fires Books Publishing

Life is really simple, but we insist on making it
complicated.

~ Confucius ~

One

ngie's gone now, but the house remains. We built it because of the views, the Blue Ridge Mountains pressing their aged backs into the denim skies above us. They're part of the Appalachian chain, reputed to be some of the oldest mountains in the world. We decided to leave the bustle and congestion of Raleigh, and Angie's romanticized excitement after seeing the western North Carolina countryside had me considering a move here. She said the mountains' undulations, curling into an imperfect circle about Asheville, looked like the backs of dragons and would protect us from the vagaries of a difficult, changing world. I wasn't on board with her protective idea then, and I'm certainly not now. But seeing the mountains on a clear spring morning inferred a permanence that was counterpoint to the caterwauling human clamor of the Raleigh area, and that was enough.

While Angie was given to hearth and yard, I suffered cabin fever there, especially during winter, anxious for spring when I could head deep into the woods, feel the pines and poplars breathing about me. Or, with my camera, make my way far enough up Pisgah Trail to try to capture the mountain landscape through a lens. Angie, on the other hand, reveled in cooking for her occasional dinner parties which led to a mountain of dirty dishes, empty wine bottles, and damped laughter as time moved toward the next morning's hours of cleanup.

But the house. No one else had built there before us, at least in recent times, and for a short while the views were all ours. Because we were on a ridge, we had a downstairs in the back, with upper and lower decks opening to that spectacular view. We had to go cheap on the interior; because of the move, neither of us was earning that much at the time. I promised Angie that as we accumulated the funds, I'd make a dream home of the place. It seemed we had hardly settled in, planted ground cover and shrubs in the back, when another low-slung western-style, cedar-sided home began to rise between us and the mountains. Then another couple came and built. Later, another. Another after that. Then the developer who sold those five quarter-acre lots cleared most of the five ridges between us and the mountains, and proceeded to build forty more homes.

I continued to bemoan the developer's land grab, but Angie was more benevolent. Late one summer afternoon as we stood under the deck awning, the sun becoming an orange memory beyond the mountains, the eleventh home under construction, she chuckled, took a sip of her Chenin Blanc, and playfully elbowed me. "You know," she said, "the odds are that out of some forty-five homes to be built here, we'll end up with great friends in at least four." She was always conscious of her Native American background, and forever imagined anyone new she encountered would notice her skin tone and take their friendship intentions elsewhere. Still, she had a needy child's attraction for anyone who did make friendly overtures, and she would do most anything for anyone she considered a friend. She tugged my arm to solicit a response, but my gaze wouldn't leave the denuded landscape, the brutal gashes the developer's backhoe and motor grader left. The two beasts sat atop a pushed-aside hillock of rock and soil, as if mechanical versions of Hannibal's elephants, waiting to descend the Lombardian Alps.

Carly and Chris bought that second home and were our first and, for the most part, our only true neighborhood friends. Both are musicians plying other skills to make ends meet. Carly's also an artist, as was Angie, although she doesn't paint quite as feverishly as she did when we met and grew close. Chris still works at an outdoor center on the Nantahala River during summers, soliciting paddlers at the Outdoor Center to take flyers for a pizza place he takes commissions from for sending diners its way.

It was one night two winters after we moved in and just before midnight, Angie and I having just finished our semi-monthly love-fest and still lying naked in each other's arms, when the phone rang.

Angie laughed. "That had better not be your mother calling again while we're in this state. How does she know we've been doing it?"

"I'm not answering," I said. I was ready for a re-run with Angie, and I resented the possibility of an intrusion. She reached across me for the phone just as a knock at the door boomed through the house.

"What the hell," I muttered.

Angie lay atop me with the phone. "Huh. Whoever it was hung up. We really do have to get caller ID, you know?"

"She," I said. "It's my mom."

"Are you going to see who's at the door? Warren, please put on your bathrobe before you go." Her exquisite smile made an appearance. "And tell your thing to take the rest of the night off. I'm calling your mother, just for spite."

I fumbled about on the floor at the end of the bed, found my robe, barely had it tied when I opened the front door to Carly and Chris, high as a pair of North Carolina pines.

"We're hungry," boomed Chris, waving his cell phone, "what's in the fridge?"

"We brought wine," said a giggling Carly, holding a bottle of red, another of white.

Angie appeared, telling Mom to shush, a finger jabbing at the mute button. "What in the world?" She unmuted, said bye, and set the phone down, eyes wide, expectant, not at all flummoxed by this late-night invasion.

Chris, red-faced and a little subdued by our state of semi-dishabille, said, "Um, we were just asking Warren if you want breakfast, and —"

"Not another word," said Angie, "I'll make breakfast." She bustled into the kitchen motioning the three of us to follow.

Chris eyed her backside, barely concealed by her nightie, then my poorly bound bathrobe. "Ah, we're not interrupting anything are we?"

"Not at all," said Angie, who winked at me from the fridge. "We were done. Quite done."

I fetched her robe, put on a pair of pants. When I returned, Angie was stirring batter for pancakes. Soon its eggy aroma rose from one skillet, bacon in another.

"Swell of you to do this," said Chris. He scratched his curly blond hair, set his thin frame on a stool at the breakfast bar.

Carly added, "Yeah, we were kidding, actually. We

didn't really expect —"

"Nonsense," said Angie. "I'll have a white. Warren, your usual red?"

I nodded, picked wineglasses from the upper cabinet while Chris opened, and before long we were wolfing down pancakes, bacon, and wine.

"So," said Angie. She made coffee and then began a new round of pancakes. "What's the occasion?"

"Wedding anniversary," said Carly, still feeling the wine and whatever else she'd had earlier.

"Not really," said a chuckling Chris.

Carly slapped playfully at his arm and said, "Okay, it's actually next week, but we thought we'd get an early start."

Chris feigned a defeated look. "In too deep to back out now."

Angie turned a wary expression to me. This was her third marriage, my second. Her first two had been economic disasters, at least that was our story when marital history became an implied topic of conversation. My first had run off with another woman six months after we married. Understandably, we entered our initial try at togetherness with due caution. We lived together for a few months, thought better of it, broke up, and a year later began dating again. "I won't do it," Angie said one night as we cautiously explored the subject of renewing our cohabitation, "unless we get married." She eyed me. "But I know you have reservations."

"No, no," I told her, forcing myself not to smile at the way she phrased that. "I'm ready this time."

She pushed me back to arm's length. "Are you sure?"

I was and said so. Hers was a coppery coloration, pretty typical of the northern New Mexico pueblo country she was born into, and she squinted a little as she evaluated my reply.

Then she nodded. She believed me.

"What?" said Carly, noticing but not able to interpret Angie's look.

"We had a couple of practice marriages," I replied.

Angie surrendered a strained smile. "Three."

"And we thought we knew you two," said Chris, giving the breakfast bar a mock fist-pound.

"Honey," said the suddenly serious Carly, "that's their business."

I was about to agree, but Angie said, "One for Warren, two for me." She set a platter high with fresh pancakes on the bar, told the three of us to split them, poured coffee all around, and continued. "My first couldn't hold a job. Pretty typical on the Navajo res; in the Taos area where we lived, not so much. Every time I thought I might go back to college, get my MFA, he would quit his job or be fired, and I'd have to keep the secretarial position I had. We divorced after three years. I met Warren at an art show there."

"Wait," said Carly, "you met Warren then? Before your second marriage?"

The conversation was beginning to unsettle me. Maybe it was Angie's dead-serious tone, something that rarely emerged, but when it did, I knew to tread cautiously. "I'm Warren the Second," I replied. "The improved model."

Angie reached, gave my hand a squeeze. "Definitely. Warren the First was rather immature. He'd take out his frustrations on me."

"No!" said Carly. "He hit you?" She descended from her stool, looped behind Angie, who stood facing Chris and me, and poured from the coffee pot.

"He wanted us to be co-breadwinners. Wanted wifey to become a paralegal, both of us to make tons of money. Live the good life. That wasn't my preference, since I had artistic aspirations and, unfortunately, he believed me when I told him so."

"He did hit you, then," Carly said. "Honey, I'm so sorry."

To my surprise, she nodded. It was deep into our second try before she told me this. Maybe women see men as inherently unable to keep a secret, or maybe Carly and Angie had, in the short time we'd known them, already achieved a deeply confiding friendship. Angie continued.

"He didn't drink or use drugs, but he'd go into these rages, you know? When he was in that state, all you could do was grimace and take the pounding. I lost a couple of teeth."

"The son of a bitch put her in the hospital more than once," I blurted, something I promised I'd never tell. But then there was this confessional conversation going on, and I couldn't help it.

She gave me a daggered look. Then it softened, eyes filled with a misty, loving sheen. "He did. I went to a battered women's shelter. They helped me take out a peace warrant, wanted me to have him arrested, but I said no. He just needed to know the law was on my side. We divorced and he went to Colorado. Never to be heard from again."

"I would've never imagined," said Carly.

"Yeah, you're one tough cookie," said Chris.

A combative energy seemed to shoot through Angie, like a thermometer set in the sun on an August afternoon. When it subsided, she smiled. "Not really so tough."

With that, I changed subject to the three new homes currently being built. Our coffee couldn't withstand the onslaught of the pancakes' carbohydrate mellowing, and we quieted. As dawn began its eastern creep, they hugged and thanked us, returned home, and Angie and I slept in one another's arms until noon.

Two

Spring of the following year. By then we'd had our fill of construction equipment lingering on the next ridge over. The backhoe had stopped, its bucket in mid-hole. It had been that way for a week, Chris told me one Saturday morning as we hiked down the French Broad River's east bank on the south side of town. I had been slugging it out with tax forms for the past week and hadn't really noticed. After all, I'd been trying to ignore the destruction aspect of construction.

"Equipment breakdown?" I asked. That was hardly likely, since the equipment seemed pretty new to me.

"Dunno. Someone's been scratching around in the mud there, and then yesterday another guy showed up, from the state apparently. Don't know what it's about."

We circled back to my Jeep, lunched at a pizza joint, and after we made a quick grocery run for Carly, found the contractor's pick-up in their drive. We found both Angie and Carly at the dining table with the house builder and another man — the state guy, as it turned out. They had a set of house plans rolled out and another, different-looking roll angled across it.

Angie introduced the contractor, Blakely. We'd heard about him but hadn't met, and then she introduced the state guy, Willard.

"What's up," I asked, "some government red tape?"

The Willard fellow bristled for a moment, then a hint of a smile. "No, a Native American site."

"What?" asked Chris. "A burial place?"

"No, honey," said Carly, "they're telling us these ridges were a Native American settlement off and on, maybe going back two thousand years. Not constantly, but over time."

I was confused. Accountants don't know much about the makings or consequent discovery of indigenous history. "But it's buried?" I asked.

"It doesn't take long for that to happen," said Willard. "Only a century or two. Vegetation grows, dies, leaves fall, there might be natural fires, and the soil builds up. From the looks of the pottery shards I've found so far in my digging, it appears to be a settlement by ancestors of the Creeks."

Angie rose, retired to the hall restroom, where I heard her cough, which always sounded like throwing up, then the godawful groaning wheezes. Carly glanced to me. I'm sure she knew what was going on, but that didn't mean I was going to air my concerns about Angie's asthma and COPD before strangers. Blakely totally misinterpreted what was going on, and that deflated the awkwardness we were all feeling.

He winked at me, said, "You need a kid in the house, you know? Always fills up the empty spaces to have a kid."

We laughed somewhat tentatively at that and then got down to business. Willard, who had been standing there like a poplar on a windless day, now turned an officious look to Blakely. "I'm afraid we're going to have to stop your work here, Marcus."

Blakely sat back, took a deep breath, and rubbed calloused hands across his temples. "You can't do that. I have loans for five homes right now and bills to pay." He looked to the four of us. "You folks want me to leave this place all torn up?"

A pause before Chris replied. "If you'll reclaim those lots, plant some shrubs, it'll be fine with us."

Carly nodded. I followed suit.

"But not before we remediate the site," said Willard.

"For Pete's sake," said Blakely. "You and your goddamn Indians are gonna put me out of business. I just bought new construction equipment. I have crews I'll have to lay off and won't ever get them back. And the bank loans…" He muttered something unintelligible, rose, rolled his plans, and stalked toward the door.

"I'm going to need that roll of land plots, the part with the topographical layouts," Willard called out.

Blakely wheeled, swept the plans from under his arm and made to throw them. Willard rose in challenge. For a tense moment, I thought we were going to have a mano a mano fight between the construction industry and State of North Carolina right there in Carly's kitchen. Blakely blew out a breath, slowly lowered his arm and handed the roll away. The front door glass rattled when he slammed it behind him.

"Was that true?" I asked Willard.

He looked up, blinking, glasses making his eyes seem oversized. "What's that?"

"What he said…going out of business," Angie gasped from the hallway entrance to the dining area. She was scrabbling about in her pocket for a fresh inhaler.

Willard chuckled. "Oh, that. Well, hopefully not. Contractors like Marcus always manage to land on their feet."

"But, I mean, do you have to put him in that position?" Carly said. "I wanted him out of here, and quickly, but not this way. "Your remediation won't take but a week or two, will it?"

"It might take from now until fall." He opened a satchel and extracted a stack of photos taken the previous week, spread them across the table. "I didn't tell Marcus, but there are other artifacts."

"You didn't tell him?" asked Carly. "Why?"

"He owns the land. He might want to keep them, and we'd have to sue to get them," Willard replied. "Judging from the depth where we're finding them, plus their nature, they're the oldest ever found in North Carolina, maybe anywhere in the east. This site is incredibly valuable, you see?"

I stood, leaned and scanned them. There were ornaments, pieces of primitive jewelry, a pair of small bowls made of shells, somehow cemented together. Bits of precisely woven wicker with an ornate design, clearly from a degraded basket. Stone and wooden tools. A large piece of tanned deer hide. The big find so far seemed to be a completely intact stone and clay oven. If these artifacts were as old as Willard imagined, people twelve hundred years ago were far more sophisticated than you'd expect.

Willard smiled. "What you couldn't know from the photos is that the signs I'm finding indicate a ceremonial and burial site nearby. These were probably an elite people within a tribal group living here. A sub-cult of priests and priestesses. Such sites are considered sacred."

"To whom?" This from Angie.

His voice rose. "To anyone. To any of the tribes nearby during the Woodland era or now. If any of the tribes found out we had trashed this site, we'd be sued. The law is now on their side when it comes to uncovering their relics." He tapped his chest with a pair of fingers. "Not the state, but me. Me personally. And my staff. You understand?"

"Look," said Chris, "I want this cleared up as fast as Blakely, get him the hell out of what I thought was my backyard before those godawful machines crawled in. Can't you bring in some other crews, you know, double your manpower?"

A huff. "No. I can't keep people at what the state pays. We'd need to bring in outside archaeologists. Maybe a couple of historians. The history is guesswork that far in the past, and the different disciplines have differing perspectives on that. It'd take a while for them to resolve their conclusions based on what we excavate."

"Okay, okay," said an irritated Chris. "Tell us what you need to tell us and get back to work."

Putting it that way to someone of Willard's ilk meant a half-hour lecture on Native American archaeology. He gave us that and then some. I was only half listening, but there was something about Paleoindians preceding Archaic ones, and then the Woodland tribes we were maybe a tiny bit familiar with. Most he mentioned were names we had never heard of — Abihka, Kashita, Kawita, Oakfuskee, speaking equally foreign languages — Muscogee, Hittite, Koasati, Yuchi.

But his last statement was the most poignant. He stowed his sketches and photos, rose, and looked to each of us in turn. "Despite your comments, you folks seem more open to what I have to do than most. To people like Marcus Blakely, it's a matter of economics. He and his people make money by building homes for folks like you. But here's the thing. These tribes I mentioned, and the older ones we know next to nothing about, they had families here too. They were part of civilizations that preceded us. Every new culture that crops up, it's influenced in some way by even older ones. The Woodlands fought the white settlers, sure, but wouldn't you? Even so, we took words from their languages, gave their names to our towns and counties. That makes them a part of us. We wouldn't just disappear mementos and records of our grandparents and great-grandparents, and we should honor these ancient people the same way."

The four of us sat silently. We continued to sit that way as he smiled, gathered his things, and said good-bye.

We heard his pickup flounce down the road and dim to a hum before Chris said, "I guess we just got a Sunday School lesson. A history lecture too." He and Carly gave us perfunctory hugs, and we returned home without further words. There, my attention turned to Angie.

"You all right, hon?" For some reason, a strange mode of humor had settled over me, which is why I stupidly added, "Blakely thought you were pregnant. You aren't, are you?"

Her eyes turned to water, and she said, "No, Warren, I'm not pregnant."

I reached for her, but she had already turned away and headed down the hall. A moment later, the bedroom door slammed and I heard her soft crying amid more coughs and COPD rasping.

Three

Curious, I waited until the weekend, when I felt sure Willard and his people wouldn't be working, and I explored their dig. I invited Angie, but she was leery, and besides, she was still suffering from asthma and a mild depression. She was born in poverty in Truchas, New Mexico, the living conditions there a tale of loss, lack, and mean streets, and she'd had double doses of pneumonia more than once, the triggers for her asthma-cum-COPD. She had barely-treated bacterial pneumonia three times, she thought, but her memory of childhood was vague on that. The resulting asthma had a deep hold on her, had been untreated until she was a pre-teen, when she went to live with her maternal grandparents in Taos. A plucky kid, certainly. Her mother was white, a prodigious boozer who had married her drinking partner, a Pueblo construction worker living in Albuquerque, more than enough reason for Angie's on-and-off depressive spells. She assured me she was feeling well enough this day, however, to be left alone to her painting, so I pulled on my boots and investigated the dig.

Dogwoods and willows were already in bloom, as were a good many flowers, including daffodils and phlox. The air contained a mixture of staid coolness and transient warmth. The sky was a pale blue Angie called Maya, with gossamer-like cirrus embedded in it. I figured I could poke around the dig a little, enough to sate my curiosity, then take a short hike. Batter boards surrounded the excavation area, and Willard's people had fastened a heavy nylon string to them with small nails. No one was around, so I climbed over and into the excavation pit. I poked into the clayey soil with a trowel, randomly at first, then in a long, straight line. Halfway through my second line, I hit something. A large stone, from the sound of it. Carefully troweling the soil away, I began uncovering a boulder with engraved markings. At first, I thought these were decorative, but the more I saw of them, the more they looked like some sort of writing.

"Hey!"

I jumped at the voice, almost fell into the pile of dirt I'd just built.

"What do you think you're doing?" yelled Willard in his tremulous voice. "You're not supposed to be in there. Didn't I tell you it was valuable?"

I stood and picked my way through the dig's up-and-down areas toward the reed-thin, balding man with the swarthy face, and climbed from the pit. "I was just curious. There's no reason to get bent out of shape."

He stomped, face flushed. "My God, man, have you ruined my dig?"

"Just poked the ground in a few places until I hit a large piece of rock, then I uncovered part of it, that's all."

"Where? Where's the piece of rock?"

"It's a boulder, actually, by the look of it." I turned and pointed.

"That's it!" he said. "That's what I've been looking for. A Cherokee legend mentioned an inscribed boulder in this area. This is so fortuitous! Did you take photos? Because if you did, you need to hand them over. They belong to the State of North Carolina."

"No photos. But it's marked in some fashion. Looks like writing."

"Of course it does," he called out. He scrambled into the pit, then bent to inspect the exposed portion of the boulder.

His certainty had me cowed. "I was careful," I mumbled. "I just scraped the dirt off it."

He spun, glaring. "With what?"

I held up the trowel.

"You use a brush!" he said. "A brush! Go to my truck. There's a metal case in the back. Get the large brush, and a couple of small ones. A spritzer bottle that's in there, too. And bring a bucket of water from your house. Now go!"

He wouldn't let me into the pit, had me hand the items to him. He cleaned the boulder's exposed portion with the care of a jeweler, then had me fetch his camera. The photography phase took almost as long as the cleaning, and by the time he climbed from the pit, he was smiling. I asked to see the pictures. He gave me a hard look, nodded, had me bring his laptop from the truck. A half-dozen of the uploaded shots moved to a separate file. We examined those under the house's top deck awning.

He tapped the last photo with a finger, and he didn't look happy. "The inscription, I don't know the language." He pushed the laptop over to me as if asking me to interpret this odd inscription. I took the laptop, held it to the light to see if there were traces of missing letter parts discernible on the boulder, or whether I might've scraped valuable parts away with the trowel. I saw nothing that wasn't obvious and handed the device back.

He shut it down, rose, and gave me a slight bow. "I'm going to have to send these photos to D.C.," he said. Another hint of a bow, he thanked me, turned away, and descended the deck steps. "Don't go in the pit again," he called out as he turned the corner toward his pickup.

A week later, my cell rang. "Someone in D.C recognized the inscription," said Willard.

"Some super-old tribe, I guess."

"In a way. The inscription is ancient Scandinavian, probably a Viking settlement over the older Native American one." He talked on for a while, telling me that from the inscription, Scandinavian adventurers had taken up with an Indian tribe, had lived out their years there. They had scuttled their longboats, to erase the temptation to turn back to Europe.

"So what's the prognosis, Doc?"

He smiled at that. "Now we have to wait for the D.C. crowd to come down, evaluate the site. Then I can go back to work on the Native American aspects I'm interested in."

"Blakely's going to have a kitten."

Another flash of a smile. "No, he won't. He's pulling up and moving across town, working for another developer. He won't be back for a year."

Willard kept the dig going until a week before Blakely returned, and three months later I received a surprise gift: a brand-new copy of *Smithsonian*, complete with pictures of the dig and a brief article that didn't reveal much, except there was more, much more to come.

Blakely made up for lost time. He took his plans for a house proposed at the dig area to an adjacent lot and finished it in four months. Building homes about us consumed most of another two years, a hectic time. Construction workers swarmed the site, stacks of building materials appeared, disappeared, then more appeared. When what seemed eternal machine noise finally ended, forty new homes dotted the ridges. Finally, the land around us began to heal, except for Willard's dig, which remained open.

Four

$\mathcal{A}$ngie and I were so glad to see the construction over and houses occupied that we barely noticed trouble brewing. The other homes formed an association to keep up the common areas, and they asked us to join them. After a modicum of discussion and hand-wringing, we decided to be included. A clique quickly formed in the neighborhood, however, its members mostly older folks from out of state, many former mid-level corporate executives and their spouses, scaling down to accommodate their retirement income. The neighborhood covenants were applied unevenly, the cliques began quarreling among themselves, and the less financially endowed among us took the brunt of the association's abuse. A few families moved out, either for economic reasons or to escape the constant bickering.

Two more years passed. Blakely had left the streets in sad shape, there were water main blowouts, the repairs left ruts, and two bad winters did more damage. The neighborhood association decided to repave. During a meeting with the three short-listed contractors, more arguments ensued. All three contractors declined to work for us, so we hired a small company hungry enough to put up with us, and they made the roads worse. Recrimination became the tone of conversation in the neighborhood. Some of the less-financially endowed families couldn't afford to re-paint their houses as quickly as the association wished. Those home owners said, "Sue me," and refused to paint at all.

There were other things, funny from my current distance, not so much then. A single woman moved in next to Carly and Chris who, when she saw Chris, would bare her chest in the nearest window. Amused, Chris told Carly, who threatened to call mental health officials on the neighbor. Then, abruptly, the woman moved out. Another couple moved in on the next ridge, who chose to do all the finish work inside their house, sleeping on the floor of one room, then another, as work progressed. An older neighborhood couple kept walking in on them in early morning while the residents were still sleeping, remarking, "Don't mind us, we just wanted to see what you're doing with the house." After much acrimony, the neighborhood hired a landscaping crew to mow, trim, and blow grass and leaves away from the roads, roadside strips and other common areas. On a certain Friday afternoon, and in retaliation for the clean-up noise, our nearest neighbor, an elderly woman, set stereo speakers in her windows to play Lawrence Welk cassettes at maximum volume.

Then there were the social gatherings. We were born to a younger generation than the oldest ones, who in their late sixties and early seventies, saw the fetes as reasons to get knee-walking drunk. One elderly gentleman, who hadn't mastered the skills necessary to hold a drink while negotiating a room with his walker, kept wetting his pants. His wife usually ignored that, her sights set on seeking me out and pinching my backside. Another woman, at an in-between age, who seemed to be in some odd relationship with an older couple, would drink heavily, fall down, and threaten to sue the nearest person, claiming he or she had pushed her.

Finally, Angie and I began to pull away. We, and others, like Carly and Chris, were still working and, for the most part, enjoying what we did. I withdrew from the current events discussion group I facilitated. It seemed that many of the participants lost their ability to think with discernment upon retirement and could only parrot the increasingly propaganda-like leavings of talk radio and talking-head TV. More time passed, and Angie quit the neighborhood book group, which usually spent fifteen minutes discussing the latest book and the remainder of their time gossiping, drinking coffee, and whispering criticism of the hostess' home and furnishings.

As some of the older residents began moving to assisted care centers, more involvement-prone residents moved in, and some became Board members. Absent from the work committee activities we had been taking part in, Angie took up knitting — something her doctor recommended to take her mind off the constant pain remaining from those earlier spousal beatings. I, on the other hand, began to read voraciously between hikes and, in need of a bit more income than my free-lance accounting work offered at the time, took employment with Chris at the Outdoor Center.

During the winter months that followed, I began to upgrade our home's interior. Blakely had gone far too cheap on the inside, and after a little over eight years of occupation, it was showing signs of wear. We decided the builder's wallpaper was too old-fashioned. I removed it, re-skimmed the walls with sheetrock compound, sanded my work and the original, inexpertly done drywall, and repainted with colors

Angie favored. She took to the yard when she felt up to it, and by mid-spring had floral beauty spread to the limits of our property. The Board held a "Yard Beautiful" contest, and Angie won.

"It wasn't all my doing, you know," she said when we returned home the night of the awards dinner. "You paid for the topsoil, lined the walkway beds with decorative stones, and hauled all that mulch. How many bags was it?"

I smiled as I retrieved a beer from the fridge. "I think I have amnesia about that. Traumatic, my love, so traumatic."

That set her into uncharacteristically shrill laughter. "No, the trauma was all the beer you claimed was a necessary part of the task."

"Gosh, you're welcome."

An arched eyebrow. "So when are you going to take out those cheapo kitchen cabinets?"

I glanced around the kitchen. "They look pretty good from here."

"I'm going to hide your hiking boots until I get new ones."

"And what reward comes with that task?"

The eyebrow's arch sharpened. "You got that last night."

I started to make light of our horizontal romp, but I thought better of it. She had been limping all day. Was that my doing, or a symptom of her increasingly poor physical condition? "Tell you what, lovely lady, if you'll agree to do the cooking, the dishes, and laundry for the next month, I'll get right on it."

"I do that already."

"Oh, right."

Something lurked behind the banter, something I

couldn't read in her eyes, the way she pursed her mouth. I was certain she wasn't particularly sick; we had taken a leisurely hike the previous afternoon.

I reached for her hand, but she was slow to give it. "Something the matter?" I asked.

Looking away, she replied, "No. Why?"

"I don't know, I guess I'm wrong, then."

"I'm tired," she said. "I think I'll lie down." She smiled, a bit too painfully, I think now, rose and made her way to the bedroom. I spent the night on the couch so she could rest peacefully without my thrashing.

The morning sun was just reaching me there when I felt the couch give a little. She sat beside me, ran a hand through my hair, and kissed an upturned cheek. "I took a sleeping pill," she said. "You could have slept beside me. You know they send me to Catatonia."

"Didn't even consider it." I pulled her down beside me, spooned into her, my arm gentle across her breasts.

"I'm sorry about that going-to-bed-early thing last night," she said. "I was really, really tired."

I rose to one elbow. "You sure you're okay?"

"Absolutely."

Over the next two days, I tried to get her to talk about what was going on with her. She would smile, turn away, and give me some silly, evasive answer.

I finally figured out it was the mild depression that had been bothering her. Her mood eventually lightened and, just as I was about to begin restoring the kitchen, her bestie from high school, Evie, and the husband, Ben, dropped in unexpectedly. As always when they came, everything else braked to a halt, but they left for a mountain cabin and a wedding anniversary weekend, and I began the kitchen redo.

"I have to cook in here," said Angie. "Cover things well if you want to eat."

The tarps I had were grungy from automotive maintenance and camping, so I had to buy new ones before I could start. Then there was unloading the kitchen cabinets, setting what I could on the dining room table, the rest packed and stored in the garage. That done, we headed to a cabinet shop, then another. Unable to find any Angie liked, we looked through catalogs and on-line, but she couldn't settle on a style. We went back to the first cabinet shop and went through their catalogs again. Angie finally decided on a simple, rustic style with a white pine finish. But they were in kits I'd have to assemble. Oh, and the floor linoleum was now all wrong. The dollar count was going to mount.

Two days later, assembling the cabinets done, I began the work of hanging them. The floor ones, though, became a challenge. All went well, since I had already taken out the plumbing fixtures, but installing new ones was another matter. The sink trap had me buffaloed. Such things take more than a single pair of hands, and I was muttering things no decent person should be heard saying. Then my shoulders slumped under the weight of Chris's hands.

"I could hear you swearing all the way down to our place," he said. "Kinda scorched my barbecue sandwich."

Carly laughed, and so did Angie. "C'mon," said Angie, "let's go to your place before he starts throwing stuff."

"Would he do that?" Carly asked.

"I don't plan to stay and find out."

"Good luck, pal," said Chris. "I'm outta here, too."

"Oh no, you don't," I said, still lying on the floor. "I need an extra pair of hands." Underscoring my request, I swung the pipe wrench over my head. I swear I didn't mean to hit him. The wrench rattled as it connected, causing a sickening thump.

Carly pounced, pinned me to the floor. Did she really think I hit him on purpose? All I can say is she punched my jaw and kicked the wrench away. Then she slapped me, hard.

I heard Angie yell for her to stop, and suddenly Carly was off me.

So here we were, Angie and Carly crying in one another's arms as a standing but wavering Chris yelled, "Son of a bitch! Whoa! Son of a bitch!" He touched his bloody forehead. The blood was now in his eye. The expletives stopped, replaced by gasps.

Carly pushed Angie away, tried to keep him from falling. He was still woozy, and she had a hard time holding him upright.

"He's in shock, I think," Angie said. "Bring him to the couch, let him lie down there."

Chris shook his head, muttered, "No, no…too much blood. Here." He slipped to his knees, onto his back, and closed his eyes.

Carly turned to me, kicked, missed. "Damn you! Do something!"

"I'll get a blanket," said Angie, "and a pillow."

"I'll get bandages," was my failsafe add to the conversation.

I returned from the bath closet with alcohol, peroxide, bandages, and cotton. Angie had covered him with the blanket. Carly cradled his head and tryied to shove the pillow underneath.

"No," said Angie, "under his feet. We don't want him to lose consciousness."

"I…I'm…okay," Chris said. "Really…am."

Angie had his wrist, lips moving as she counted. "His pulse is coming down."

Carly, now at his feet, began to cry.

"Not helping," said Chris. "Shut up."

"We're trying to save you," Carly screeched.

"Don't need to," he said, his voice stronger, eyes open. He struggled onto his elbows, blinking and fashioning a weak smile. "See? Better."

"Here," Angie said to him, "let me treat that cut."

"No, I'll do it." Carly, still crying, snatched the peroxide-soaked cotton. Then, suddenly, she calmed and began cleaning the wound, reaching like a seasoned nurse for the pair of butterfly bandages Angie held. That done, Chris asked for water, then coffee, and minutes later Angie, Chris, and I were talking and laughing. Not Carly. She kept turning her dour look to me and said nothing. Finally, she forced a smile and said to Chris, "I better get you home, honey."

"Not on your life," he replied. "I came over here to help my pal. That's what I aim to do."

I looked to Angie, then Carly and Chris. "I think I'm done for the day. Better if you rest, don't you think?"

After supper, the phone rang and Angie answered. Carly told her Chris was okay. She had calmed down, no doubt at his insistence. She apologized for hitting me, but she didn't want Chris at our place helping me with the plumbing. The next day, everything went together like clockwork, the countertop guy delivered that, and Angie and I unloaded the garage boxes and placed pots, pans, and cleaning supplies in their new homes.

Five

One Saturday morning the following February, Angie and I were sitting in the kitchen drinking a second cup when the phone rang — someone I wouldn't have expected. "Willard!" I said, laughing, "Don't tell me you want to dig up the neighborhood again."

"Then you heard," he replied. He had only been to our dig sporadically since the *Smithsonian* article.

"I'm going to clean out my closet," said Angie. "Or something." She topped off her coffee and, still in her pajamas and robe, trundled off to the bedroom.

"It started," said Willard, "with the pool."

I knew some of the neighbors wanted to have an in-ground pool built, but the assessment would be huge. Angie and I had missed the last two Board meetings, part of our edging away from neighborhood politics. The neighborhood remained a contentious lot, including some of the more recent move-ins. Too many wanting to boss the rest, basically. Some were claiming others were getting preferential treatment from the Board, others didn't seem inclined to abide by neighborhood covenants.

As Willard talked, I absently opened a drawer, noticed an old receipt from CVS for some prescriptions I'd paid for a neighbor three houses down. The resident, a woman, had contracted cancer. Her divorced husband had volunteered to move in and take care of her.

"We barely know the woman," I suggested when Angie mentioned that we should help her.

"Neighbors are neighbors," she said. "I'd like to know, if it were you and me, that we had some neighbors we could rely on to help us out." The next morning, she cooked some mashed potatoes, a green bean casserole, and made a loaf of sourdough bread. I bought flowers and a GET WELL SOON balloon, arranged an account at CVS for med cost help, something I would cover the cost of, bought the guy a six-pak of local beer, and we trooped over to their house looking like a combo of Welcome Wagon and the Ringling Brothers-Barnum & Bailey Circus. The man let us in. Without a word, he led us to the kitchen, where he was preparing to clean out his wife's tracheostomy and IV line.

"Some neighbors," he said to his ex, "brought food and flowers." Eyes closed, she didn't move. He performed the cleaning as professionally as any nurse. We thought she was asleep as he did this, but upon finishing, she opened her eyes, took us in, and began to cry, muttering hoarsely.

"She said you're so kind," he translated. "I can't tell you how much we appreciate your thoughtfulness. The doctor told us cancer patients tend to become isolated, and that's the worst thing for them. If there's even a borderline prognosis, the patients always seem to improve if others around them show they care. And you care. Thank you."

I misted up at that, replied with some modest words. Surprisingly, Angie, who had masterminded the whole thing, stood silent and mute. Then she elbowed me and nodded toward the door. I told the guy about the CVS account, and when I gave him bag with the beer, I thought he was going to cry, too. He hugged us both. On our walk home, I asked Angie, "What was that silent treatment all about?"

She said nothing and kept walking.

"Angie?"

"What?"

"For crying out loud, you could have shown a little sympathy. After all, helping them was your idea."

She stopped, turned, and glared at me as if we were about to do battle. Then she softened, head down, and stalked toward the house. That night she told me being confronted with the woman's condition reminded her of the way her alcohol-consumed mother had died, alone and suffering cancer, without money, insurance, or family, except for a teen Angie.

Our neighbor died a month later, and most of the residents turned out for the funeral. I wondered why some of them didn't show up when she was sick.

But back to Willard's call and the neighborhood pool issue. We figured it would be voted down. Strange, but Carly and Chris had only been over a couple of times in the past month, and they hadn't mentioned that it was a done deal. Strange, too, because they were living hand to mouth, and the assessment would knock the bottom out of their budget.

"It's to be on the east side of the development, by the road," said Willard, "where Blakely decided he won't build. From what your Board chairs are telling me, it's to be Olympic-sized. And there'll also be a clubhouse."

"Wait, wait," I said, "a clubhouse too? Where will that be?"

"Adjacent to the in-ground pool. The builder will have to bring in dirt, construct a berm to set it on. But your Board wanted to have me mitigate the site archaeologically before approving funds."

Ah. A smart move. And a window of hope. "Here's hoping you find a whole city there."

Willard chuckled at that, but it seemed a forced one. "I did take the job," he said. "I didn't want to, though. You see, I have something of a conflict."

"Conflict? I thought you loved digging in the dirt."

"Well, I didn't want to say anything before, but this one hits a little too close to home. I had family living nearby. Not the Creeks, that would be right up my alley. But what came after that."

That was too vague for me to comment on, so I grunted noncommittally.

"Look, the reason I'm calling is I need a second opinion on something. *Smithsonian* wanted more about my dig, so I'm writing a rather extensive paper about the site, and I'd like to have someone read the first of it, someone who might be sympathetic to my thinking before sending it on. Would you be willing to do that, see what you think, from a reader's standpoint?"

I have to say I was intrigued, but what did I know about archaeology? Anyway, I said I would, and he rang our bell an hour after we hung up, the first few chapters in a manila envelope he held under one arm. He beamed as if he'd just won a Pulitzer, turned abruptly and left before either of us could exchange pleasantries. Angie was still clumping around in her closet, so I repaired to the den. I only had to read the second sentence before my jaw dropped.

"Just north of Asheville, North Carolina, and a few miles from Tennessee, sits Catawba Corners Subdivision, land that once belonged to the Creek Indians many, many years ago. More recent times saw it in the hands of my great-great grandfather Herbert Rose's great-great grandfather, Hiram, both on my mother's side, who came up the Broad River with three associates into what had once been disputed territory between the French and English. He brought a flatboat laden with blankets, flour, coffee, cooking utensils, and knives, hoping to trade for furs with indigenous people. When the boat could go no farther, somewhere in what is now South Carolina, he hired six Cherokees with mules to pack the goods overland and into the mountains. On the trek, it quickly became clear that the Cherokees were wary of Hiram and his three companions, not to mention the prospect of meeting bands of the hated Catawbas. A drought and natural fires, however, had taken much of the life from this territory over the previous years. Most remaining game had migrated to what is now Tennessee."

Willard's paper read easily. It wasn't academic; it was more nearly journalism, drawn, I supposed, from his archaeological studies and digs and supplemented by historical readings. Native tribes in the area had, for a few hundred years, settled in select spots throughout the mountains, but internecine warfare, drought, and game migration had set them afoot again. Unused to the rigors of the constant wandering, many died. Tribes, from large to moderate to small, dissolved their associations and moved west and south, leaving only a few marauders. Willard's reporting went on at length to depict this, and then he set Hiram's exhausted band of traders at the headwaters of what is now the French Broad River.

Hiram, according to his description of the trek, insisted his companions not eat too heartily from their few food supplies, hoping to trade most of it for beaver pelts and deerskins, and so they subsisted largely off the land, eating occasional raccoons and opossums, the Cherokees opting for rabbit and an occasional fish. A raccoon the three friends ate, apparently diseased, poisoned one. He died, then another. The next night, three of the Cherokees and the remaining partner left with most of Hiram's trading goods. Finally, one mid-afternoon, he stumbled on a small clan of Catawbas encamped on a series of ridges near what is now Asheville, North Carolina, some twenty miles south of the Tennessee line.

The village was strung out across the nexus of two ridges, their lodges dome-shaped affairs flattened at opposite ends to provide entrances. Some of these openings were covered with woven grasses, others simply draped with sewn-together animal skins. At the joining point of the two ridges, halfway down the slope, lay a flattened area with a circle of large stones, a boulder at its center, perhaps an altar of some sort, Hiram assumed. A few feet farther down, at the ridge's base, a glowing fire burned and crackled. In a swale between the ridges, a large, terraced garden lay in waves across the bottomland. Canes of the previous year's stunted corn rose above the forbidding soil, along with dried-up vines, probably of beans, squash, and melons. Even with the drought, weeds had claimed the spaces between the mounded rows.

Hiram's decimated band emerged from the trees into the Catawba clearing, but upon seeing the beggared village, two of the Cherokees backed away, slipped through the trees to the east and headed toward southerly Carolina. The last one, an older man, who was Hiram's guide, tried to wave him off the ridges, but Hiram refused. He stumbled toward the Catawba encampment and called out. Several of the tribal group scrambled to their feet, brandished knives and stumbled toward Hiram. His guide, realizing he couldn't run, followed Hiram, shouting out in the Catawba dialect.

Great enmity lay between Cherokee and Catawba, and two of them seized Hiram's guide. One, a young man with what seemed to have once been a muscular build, grabbed Hiram's guide by his hair, brandished a knife, and was about to cut his throat when an elderly woman hobbled up, yelling to put the knife away. The man did, grudgingly. The old woman, a respected shaman, or priestess within the clan, conversed briefly with the Cherokee, told him her name was Broken Wing.

He turned to Hiram. "She said you shouldn't be here. They're poor and cannot feed you."

Hiram noticed their clothes were a patchwork of deerskins sewn together. The few children took him in through blank eyes. Their abdomens protruded. A few older men had only patches of hair remaining. Only the women seemed relatively fit. "Tell 'em," Hiram said, "that I'll share what we have. That it's too far to return to the Tah-kee-os-tee River right now. We'd like to stay for a short while and rest our weary bones."

The old Cherokee frowned. "You should not do that, Hiram. They will kill us both."

But Broken Wing had heard the Cherokee name for the Broad River. She moved between the two, spoke to the Cherokee, who studied the woman for a moment before replying in animated fashion. She nodded toward Hiram and, through the Cherokee, said, "Tell the white man that you may both stay until the sun returns. But tell him you must sleep downwind. You smell bad."

The next morning, the Cherokee gathered firewood, and Hiram, remaining an undaunted salesman, unpacked his remaining mule and set out his wares and provisions. He and the Cherokee built a cooking fire. Hiram brought out hardtack, salt pork, a measure of spices, and coffee. The Cherokee made a stew with the pork and spices and added some herbs of his own. The Catawbas gathered about the fire peering at Hiram's foodstuffs. The old woman spoke.

"They haven't eaten in three days," the Cherokee told Hiram.

He frowned. "Nothing?"

"Look at them. They will die soon. They may decide to kill us. Eat us."

Hiram studied the gathered Catawbas then said, "Build another fire. We'll cook a third of what we have and feed 'em. Better'n them eating us, eh?"

The Cherokee explained to Broken Wing that Hiram would feed them, and as the words registered, wary smiles emerged. The cooked food quickly disappeared. Some who ate too quickly stumbled into the nearby trees and threw up. But the food was good, and Hiram had a pair of the women cook more of his stores in their own way.

In early afternoon, clouds scudded in from the south. Rain began to fall. A wave of excited murmuring wove through the Catawbas. A few set out animal-skin buckets to collect water. Hiram was about to gather his remaining pots and pans, but the Cherokee shook his head and pointed to the Catawbas' containers. Hiram nodded, understanding. He would use his wares to collect water, too. Then the two took to the woods to sleep under a canvas tarp spread across overhanging branches.

The next morning, the Cherokee re-built their cooking fire. Hiram made coffee, the Catawbas already gathering about them. He made a great show of tasting his coffee, made a face, then handed his cup to the Cherokee, and whispered to imitate him. He tasted and shook his head. Hiram took the cup, spooned in a mound of sugar, tasted it, smiled, and handed it away. This time the Cherokee smiled and nodded. Hiram poured another, added sugar, and offered this cup to one of the Catawbas. The man sipped, grinned, and spoke fervently.

"It's the best thing he's ever tasted," the Cherokee told Hiram.

He was about to tell the Cherokee to offer the others some of the coffee, but they were already passing the cup among them. Then something caught his eye beyond the gathering at woods edge. "Tell 'em," he said, "not to make any sudden moves and not to turn around, just move real easy like a few steps to the left." The Cherokee gave him an odd look. "Just do it," said Hiram, and the old man complied. Hiram talked to his guide in a low voice as he slowly picked up his musket, loaded and tamped it. He fired. The old woman was the first to turn. She saw the elk buck fall, and as he slumped into the brush, she began to sing something that sounded like an incantation.

A few of the men ran to the elk, whooping as they ran. They cut the animal's throat where it lay, bled it, tied its feet together with nearby vines, hacked away a sturdy sapling and hauled the corpse back to Hiram's fire. The old woman continued her incantation. When she was done, she gave the crowd a long speech, occasionally motioning in Hiram's direction.

"What's she saying?" he asked the Cherokee. "Do we

need to skedaddle?"

"She's saying that the Yehasuri like you," the Cherokee replied. "The spirit people like that you have fed the Catawbas, and so they have sent rain. They like that you are peaceful, that you have not threatened them, and so they have rewarded the people with this elk. And, despite your bringing a Cherokee into their midst, the spirits have decided to reward you as well. They are proud of you and your hunting prowess. They wish for you, and me, if Broken Wing is agreeable, to stay for as long as we wish. And she is."

Willard's paper went on to describe the next year of Hiram's life spent among the Catawbas. He married a young woman of the clan. But yearning for company with his own kind, he gathered his things and prepared to leave. He returned to his wife and her clan two months later with more goods.

In this way, he began a profitable trade with his wife's clan and other native groups, which were returning to the increasingly verdant land nearby. Game once again grew plentiful. Corn stood tall and erect in the swale between the ridges.

The partial manuscript Willard had given me ended there. I sent him a rather long e-mail, telling him the aspects of his story I liked best and, generally, that I found these early chapters captivating.

For a while during the following days, I forgot about Willard's story; despite our earlier withdrawal from the neighborhood drama, Angie and I were drawn back in. I, however, took two steps forward with her, then a step back, and let her wade in as deeply as she wished. The neighborhood families were feuding with one another over the Board's decision to build the pool and clubhouse. Older residents wanted the pool so they could bring their grandkids there to swim during summer vacation. Others said, no, it should be for residents only, and besides, we can't swim with twenty brats splashing away. Others balked at the potential cost of the project. Angie and Carly tried to sort out the conflict during Board meetings, but Angie was having nerve problems in her legs, stemming from childhood trauma, she told me as it worsened. So we dropped out of neighborhood involvement again. We spent a lot of time at her neurologist's office, she submitting to tests, some rather painful.

Six

One afternoon, on the way to the neurologist's, Angie began crying. I pulled over in a strip mall parking lot and tried to hug her. She swore and pushed me away. Whenever she was like this, if comfort wasn't working, I'd try levity. I don't remember exactly what I said, but I got her reply in a hand-on-my-face manner. She'd never slapped me before; in fact, I can't remember a single time she'd truly been angry with me. We were never like that; as with most couples, we'd go through the tension of a spat, then everything would be healed. My reply to the slap: "I guess I didn't think that through, did I?"

Instead of her usual wrinkled nose and smile at my self-deprecatory joke, tears flooded her face, shiny liquid crystals that grew within themselves, spreading across her cheeks and coruscating as they fell onto her blouse's collar.

"I'm so sorry," she wailed. "I have things on my mind."

"Things? What things, hon?"

"Just things."

It sounded like something she'd never mentioned, and I knew it was futile to start probing.

Of course, she knew I wanted to, so she said, "Things I can't share right now."

That burrowed deeply into me. For the first time ever, I felt an urge to yell at her. I knew it was the slap's sting, followed by this non-revelatory comment. I took a deep breath and let it pass, put the car back in gear and drove on. Her doctor's office was just ahead, Angie still crying.

The moment I parked, she threw open the car door and rushed in. I sat in the car for a while thinking. What was going on with her? We always talked about everything, at least I thought we did. Was she having an affair? That hardly seemed likely. She was almost always home, and so was I. Even when she went to the grocery or shopping, there was no lost, unaccounted-for time. I played the incident over in my thoughts, then sampled a couple of her absences from the house. No, it couldn't be an affair, so what is it she feels she can't share? I came up empty. Totally empty. Finally, I climbed out, locked the car, and was about to open the lobby door, when she pushed it open. She smiled uneasily and said, "Doctor Phelps wants to talk."

"All right," I said, sure I had to somehow defend myself against something. "Do I need to make an appointment?"

"It's not about you," she said. "He wants to talk about me. Right now."

I think I turned a little red at my thickheadedness as I followed her through the lobby, into the labyrinth of narrow corridors to a small suite at the building's rear. Phelps stood inside by his receptionist's desk, leafing through a magazine. He looked up, smiled, and motioned us into his cubbyhole office. We were almost elbow to elbow, and I found the overage of intimacy uncomfortable.

"It seems something's arisen in our visit today that Angie's keeping from you but feels she shouldn't," he said.

My face flushed again. It wasn't proving to be a good

day for me. "I guess I didn't realize how much the pain, the cramps, the poor sleep were getting to her, Doc. We had a discussion of sorts on the way over —"

"She told me she slapped you."

For a moment I didn't know how to respond. "Well, yeah, but it's no big deal. She clearly meant no harm, and I'm already over it." That was untrue, but I was speaking into the future. I would remember the slap, but the sting and my anger were already gone.

"I'm afraid Angie hasn't forgotten it," he replied. "My field is neurology, but there's often a psychological component that comes up when long term pain is an issue, especially if it occasionally becomes intense. And in Angie's case, it has been."

"The slap wasn't a big deal, really," I insisted. "It was just that one time —"

"Please, Warren," said Angie, "will you please listen?"

She and Phelps held evaluating gazes on me, as if this were an intervention and I the problem. "Look, I just want to help."

"And you're going to have to, I think," said Phelps. "There are deeper issues involved than simply her pain, and I'm already way out of my wheelhouse with this." He reached for a prescription pad and scribbled something. He tore off the sheet and handed it to Angie, who handed it to me. Nothing there but a name: Bernard Walcott.

"What's this?"

"Oh, for Pete's sake," said Angie.

"It's a referral," Phelps said. "A counselor. He has some psychological training that I don't have."

"Is there anything more either of you can tell me about

this right now?" I asked, wondering if this hidden subject was going to set the woods on fire between us.

Angie was about to say something, but Phelps gave his half-an-answer: "You two apparently aren't communicating well with one another about certain, important things, it seems." He jabbed an arched finger my way, and then waved it at the piece of paper. "Dr. Walcott can help. He has a lot of experience, and he's very capable." He nodded toward the door. "He's right down the hall."

Still the gaze, from both of them. Angie's expression seemed a combination of eagerness and fear, but she said nothing more. Phelps' expression was a bit bemused, flustered, perhaps, at the position he seemed to have put himself in.

"This what you want?" I asked. "For us to go into counseling?"

"It's what we need," she said, giving me a look of certainty I hadn't seen much of recently.

Phelps glanced at his watch and smiled, asked if Angie had any final questions or comments. The whole thing from the slap to Phelps' comment about our ability to communicate had blindsided me. I needed time to think. She said no, no other concerns at this time, and Phelps followed us into the anteroom, where an elderly man awaited his session.

Seven

Angie made an appointment with the Walcott fellow, and two weeks later we sat in his tiny waiting room passing time. He called Angie in, and the door remained closed for almost an hour. Then he opened and asked me in. He kept looking to us, then to a yellow legal pad, apparently his notes. A moment later, he smiled. "So, Warren, may I call you that?"

"If you like." For some reason, I was feeling defensive.

"Good, good. And how do you feel about all of this?"

"Well, I'm not sure what it is," I replied, with a glance to Angie. No hint there about what had transpired between them, except her makeup was a bit smeared — evidence of crying?

Walcott frowned. "Oh? I was under the impression that you had some concerns with Angie's personal history."

Another glance to Angie, who remained impassive but maybe a little sheepish. "Her personal history? That she came from a Native American father and a white mother isn't remotely a problem between us. Never has been." Another glance. Angie was now twisting in her seat, her expression growing even more sheepish.

Walcott's frown grew. "Angie?"

She started crying, and it took a couple of minutes for that to pass. "You'll hate me if you know," she said in a mewling voice.

I reached for her hand. She pulled away, but finally let me take it. I brushed a sprig of hair from her face and started to say something, what, I don't remember, but Walcott shook his head, so I remained silent. She glanced to him, said, "I didn't mean to mislead you Dr. Walcott, it's just that I've never talked about all that before and, well, I thought if you had the idea that Warren knew about it…"

It? What the hell was going on? She squeezed my hand a few times, wiped tears away, and gave me one of her engaging smiles.

"…then I could tell him at some point, you know, when I felt the time was right, but then you wanted to bring him into it, so I was sort of caught, you know?" She launched into a story so unlike my knowledge of her that my mouth hung open.

It was the depth of winter in Albuquerque, and Angie heard her bedroom door open. She had gone to bed with her clothes on, a naked pillow and a thin blanket her only refuge from the cold in the shabby duplex apartment. Her father's footsteps lumbered across the linoleum flooring. She had her eyes open and was staring at the wall beside her bed, her back to the door. From the sound of those unsure steps, he was still drunk, had probably stayed up drinking deep into the night. If he'd slept at all, it had been while passed out.

"Angie," she heard, but didn't move. As far as he was concerned, she was still asleep.

This time he gave her a shove, called out louder. "Angie!"

"What?"

A chuckle. "I knew you weren't asleep, baby. Now turn over and give Daddy a kiss." This was a re-play of something that had happened a month earlier, the day she turned thirteen.

"No."

"Aw, c'mon, baby, you're gonna make me mad."

He pulled her blanket away, turned her face up, her eyes now closed. She felt his hands, then her pants were around her knees. The weight of him, his arrhythmic movement, the smell of sour mash and cigarettes as he clumsily kissed her. I won't cry, she thought, but then she did.

"Did I hurt you, baby?" he cooed in his raspy voice. "I didn't mean to. You know I love you, don't you know that?"

No! she wanted to scream. You don't love me! You wouldn't do this if you did.

Now, in Walcott's office, she was crying. He handed me a box of tissues. I set them on Angie's lap. She slapped it away.

"You sure you want to keep going?" I asked, and took her hand. She squeezed it briefly, then let go.

"I think you understand what she wants to share with you," Walcott said to me. A throat clearing before he said, "Angie, you've accomplished what you set out to do. It might be best to stop now."

"Stop?" she screeched. "How am I supposed to do that? He never stopped. He did it, then he did it again the next night. Then again a couple of days later. *He* never stopped!" Her crying grew louder.

I reached for her hand again, but Walcott shook no. For a while, Angie sobbed. I sat, uncomfortably rigid, while Walcott scribbled on his note pad. The crying wound down, and she looked about for the tissue box. I retrieved it, handed it to her. She mimed the words thank you, and for a moment her head bowed, eyes closed.

"Are you okay, Angie?" Walcott asked.

She nodded. "But I want to finish."

"I'm not sure that's a good idea today."

"Well, I'm going to."

From what she told me, it stopped for a while, then happened again early one morning a month later. This time she didn't cry quietly; she bawled. From her parent's bedroom, she heard muffled noises, then soft footsteps.

"Henry." Her mother's voice.

"Go away," the father bellowed.

"Henry."

A deafening noise in the small room, and a smell of something burning. Henry groaned and slumped, lifeless on top of her.

"Get him off me!" Angie screamed. She wriggled, but couldn't dislodge him. Her mother grappled with the dead body, Angie still screaming. Finally she rolled him to the floor.

The mother, Shirley, tried to hug her, but Angie shoved her away.

"I'm so sorry, honey," said Shirley.

"Go to hell! Why did you let him keep doing that?"

The doorbell began to ring insistently, then pounding and a male voice. Police. The tenant in the duplex's other side had heard Angie's screams, then the shot, and called the police. A squad car sat less than a block away. The apartment door was unlocked. The cop opened and strode in. Shirley handed him the pistol. Without protest, she allowed him to cuff her, and another cop took her away. The first one stayed until a social worker arrived. This woman talked softly and lovingly, calmed Angie, then took her to a women's shelter, where she stayed while Shirley was arraigned. The neighbor and first cop testified, which didn't go well for Shirley. But the jury sided with her, and she went free. Six months passed before she was allowed to see Angie again. Six more months elapsed before they were allowed to live together, and only after Shirley's counselor assured the court she was making significant progress in coping with her drinking.

Angie had scooted her chair against mine. Done with her story, her head slipped to my shoulder.

"Warren," said Walcott, "this wasn't the way or the time I would have preferred to have this come out, but Angie was most insistent. It would have been better to have worked much of it out between the two of us, but now I'm afraid you'll need to be a partner in our work together."

I told him that was fine; in fact I would have had no idea what was worrying Angie otherwise. He talked to Angie again alone for a while, and on the drive home, she asked, "Do you still love me?"

"Of course. Always."

For the rest of the drive, she remained silent, her forehead against the rider's side window.

Eight

$\mathcal{A}$ month later, in early afternoon, the doorbell rang. I thought it was probably one of the neighbors involved in the pool project and wanting to talk with Angie. Someone, probably Carly, had persuaded her to be on the committee. The neighborhood had broken into two sometimes angry advocacy groups, one promoting the idea that the pool and clubhouse were essential to neighborhood property values, the other advocating just as strenuously against it and the assessment that had ballooned as the pool and clubhouse proposal grew flesh. Angie agreed to mediate between the warring factions and, in the end, I supported her decision, even though I knew it would up her stress level. She was at the grocery now, and I started to ignore the summoning bell. Still, for Angie's sake, I closed down my laptop, rose and answered.

It was Willard. He had a set of plans rolled up under one arm and directed downward toward my feet like a spear. His other held a large, black portfolio, the kind suitable for holding flat posters or Styrofoam display boards. "Might I come in?" he asked.

I led him to the den. "If that's about the pool and

clubhouse property, Angie's not home yet. You know she's on that committee, right?"

"Didn't know that," he replied, "but it's you I hope to have a few words with."

I pointed him toward the couch and took the recliner. He didn't sit immediately; instead, his back to me, he began unloading the portfolio onto our couch and extracted a stack of display boards, colorfully decorated, from what I could already see. Then he pulled out a collapsible tripod easel. I couldn't help a quiet smile. For reasons I never fathomed, Angie couldn't stand the guy. I have to admit there was something about this nerdy fellow that could nettle you. But at the same time, something about his obsession with the ridges always managed to capture my attention. "What in the world are you doing?" I asked.

He turned, looked to me over his glasses. "I'm sorry, I should have asked before I dragged all this out."

"It's fine, I'm curious, that's all."

"It's just that this means a lot to me, and you've been open to the history of this place, and —"

"It's okay. Really."

He's actually a good artist; he placed board after board on the easel, explaining each in detail. The first contained colored drawings depicting his vision of the dilapidated village his forebear revived on these ridges. Then one meant to show the village reconstructed and expanded in subsequent years as the population grew. He showed similar drawings of their vegetable gardens.

Hiram had sent the old Cherokee back to the coast with a monstrous pile of deerskins to trade for seeds, shoes and other clothing items, pots and pans, bolts of heavy cloth, yarn, seeds for planting, and three old but dependable rifles, along with powder, wadding, and lead for rifle balls. Along with seeds for food, he wanted cotton seed. One board showed a large cotton field in full flower.

Hiram's plan was, in a hyphenated word, self-sufficiency. The clan members, under Hiram's direction, planted and harvested the food crops, cultivated and picked the cotton. Willard displayed more drawings, these showing clan women sitting behind homemade spinning wheels, twisting the cotton into yarn and thread, which other women were weaving into cloth on large, outdoor looms. Vats had been dug into the earth and filled with water and various plant leaves to make dyes. Other vats were used for dying the cloth, all protected from sun and rain by sheds of poles lashed together and topped with layers of pine boughs.

Then a new series of boards showed log houses similar to those whites were building in the lowlands. These, Willard told me, were to house the larger extended families. Beyond, were the dome-shaped huts that were available to loner types, those who couldn't get along with family members, a few newlyweds, some huts for the ailing, and a few for visitors, traders, and itinerants. Finally, a merchandising building, as Willard called it, complete with windows. An early frontier version of a general store. One panoramic, triple-foldout board showed the complete village complex spread along the ridges, their farm in between (you could hardly call it a series of gardens at this point). At the nexus of the ridges, the store and a large oval-shaped ceremonial area. Around the periphery of the ceremonial, he'd colored in little black rectangles. I asked what those were, and he told me graves. Graves where prominent members of the clan were buried.

"Including Hiram?" I asked.

"I'm not sure. He left at one point, but I've never been

sure where he was buried, so he might have come back. He seemed to treasure the place. Toward the end of his life his writing turned to scribbling, and then his son, Andrew, took up the record-keeping. It's in another volume."

"I have to hand it to you, Willard, you have quite a vision of what it was like here back then."

"Oh, it's not that much of a vision," he said. "It's what I came up with in my research."

I grew suspicious at this point. I've always thought historians, archaeologists, and the like have overwrought imaginations. Rather than stick to the facts their research reveals, I figured they slant their data to create the past the way they want it. Willard had discovered Hiram's existence after his mother died. She kept documents, including Hiram's hand-me-down writings, in a family safe deposit box, and I was suspecting Willard wanted his story to be larger than life.

"Come on," I replied, "you can't know that. You haven't done that much digging here. All you've uncovered so far is a portion of the burial and ceremonial area, and that was about much older Indian settlements."

A rumble as the garage door opened. A moment later, the kitchen door creaked wide. Angie huffed her way in and across the kitchen with two large bags. "I'll be there to help in a sec, hon," I called out.

She appeared in the doorway to the living room, frowned at the sight of Willard. "I'll get them in, you entertain your friend. But you can help put them up if he's about to leave."

That seemed a little rude, but clueless Willard took no obvious offense. Still, a preemptive word of apology would be good, I considered. "Sorry, Willard, we interrupted you. Go ahead."

"It grew to be a central spot for these mountains," he went on, "kind of an economic and travel oasis. At a time when things were pretty primitive for Native Americans elsewhere in the area."

What he shared was interesting, I had to admit that, but he was making Hiram seem like a frontier Second Coming. So I decided to renew my challenge to his work. "How could you possibly know this much detail about what was here? For that matter, how do you even know there was a village of this size and sophistication here?"

His usual, goggle-eyed look turned cautious. "Well, it's in his notes. Hiram's diaries speak of it just this way. He had a series of notebooks, diaries, if you will. He had more education than you might think, and he was a pretty good artist. He described the place in detail, and he drew sketches." He took out a small metal case, opened it, showed me one of the tattered volumes, carefully turning the brittle, fading pages for me. Sure enough, the sketches looked pretty much like the boards.

Angie's clatter in the kitchen was growing louder. That was my cue to end Willard's presentation and help her, but he beat me to it. He apologized for the overlong presentation and began to pack his visual aids. That done, I helped him carry them to his car and thanked him for such an interesting presentation.

I began helping Angie put away the foodstuffs, both of us silent. This was the way things were between us now; she still ashamed of her childhood trauma and afraid I might make something of it, I not really knowing what I could say about them that wouldn't set her off. The two of us stood side by side stowing the last of the perishables in the refrigerator when she said rather loudly, "Why did you invite that archaeologist here?"

"I didn't. He just showed up."

She turned back, found a place for a head of cabbage on the bottom shelf. "What did he want?"

"Well, you heard, I'm sure. He's still researching this area. Seems someone in his family line lived here, kept diaries of his life."

She shut the fridge, retrieved two cups from the cupboard, poured the morning's coffee remainder for the two of us. "Do you think he's all right? In the head, I mean. Not many would be as persistent as he is about this neighborhood and his dig here."

"He's a little quirky, I guess, just passionate about his work."

"Do you think he's on the level with you? I mean, why's he telling you all this?"

"I haven't figured that one out yet."

She warmed a pair of sweet rolls, handed me one on a paper towel. "I don't want him here again, Warren. You're just encouraging his obsessions."

The sweet roll had raisins embedded in it, and the sugar and cinnamon glaze was delicious. If we weren't having this mildly testy conversation, I'd have wolfed it down and had another. The perfect complement to Angie's coffee. Instead, I nibbled. "Willard's hurting nothing. He just needs a sounding board for his findings. Did you notice the presentation boards he made up? Probably going to make a talk on it at the Smithsonian."

"I still don't want him here."

Something snapped in me. Her irrational and stubborn dislike for Willard set me off. I exploded, threw the sweet roll across the kitchen, where it stuck between a pair of the

Venetian blind slats over the sinks. "What the hell is your problem?" I yelled. "He did just show up, but his project is interesting, and I don't give a damn whether it's true or not. So come on, tell me what your problem is with Willard."

When I threw the sweet roll, her eyes went wide. She backed against the fridge, gasping for breath. I never got my answer from her. I reached for her, and to my surprise, she fell into my arms, sobbing. I stroked her hair and told her how sorry I was that I'd gone off like that. Then she pushed me away, drew back, and punched me in the nose. Blood spurted, then began to drool down my face, across my lips and chin onto my shirt. Horrified, she stumbled away, tripped, and fell. I reached to help her up, but she scrambled away like a turtle on a slippery surface, managed to gain her feet, and ran to the bedroom. Then she was in the garage. I heard the garage door open and the car crank. Tires squealed as she sped off.

I couldn't breathe. My nose was still bleeding, and clots were forming there. To make matters worse, blood was dribbling into my mouth, and the salty, metallic taste did nothing to calm me. I remembered that lying down would help, so I made my way to the den, lay down on the couch, my head hanging over the edge, legs up the backrest, feet in the air. The bleeding did stop after a while, only to begin throbbing. If I hadn't been the recipient of Angie's small, almost dainty fist and the damage it caused, I wouldn't have believed she could do that to another person, much less me. If she hadn't taken the Jeep, I would've been in the urgent care center, getting patched up.

I'm not sure now, but I think I passed out for a few minutes. Then the garage door rolled up, and she walked in with a CVS bag laden with medical supplies. The bag hit the floor under my head, and she sat on the floor beside me.

"Does it hurt?"

"Uh huh. You pack big punch."

She reached for the sack, unwrapped something, gently pushed it into one nostril. It cracked, and I could feel and smell an astringent liquid of some sort. Soon, the throbbing abated and there was no more blood. I asked for a tissue.

"Not yet," she said. "If you use one, the bleeding will start again and I'll have to do this all over."

"What'd you hit me with, brass knucks?"

She laughed softly, said, "Don't talk. Count to a hundred and sit up. Slowly."

I complied. She squirted something up my nose, and the blocked nostril opened. Then she took my hand, sat beside me, and leaned her head onto my shoulder.

"I'm so sorry," she said.

'S'okay."

"Does it still hurt?"

"Nah, was fun."

Big laughter this time. We sat like that for a while, the first time we'd had even that level of intimacy in a couple of months. "Hot tea?" she asked.

"Coffee," I replied.

She gave my hand a squeeze, rose, and sauntered into the kitchen. Soon I heard gurgling, and then the rich, nutty aroma of her Arabica coffee found me.

Nine

"**R**eally?" I made an airplane of the letter and sent it darting toward the trash can. Angie was in the kitchen, too, making banana bread and, following my shout, she turned to me at the breakfast bar.

"What?"

I jabbed a finger at the paper plane where it lay, fuselage and left wing to the floor, a foot from the trash can. "Your neighborhood association. The letter. Read it."

She picked it up, and as she unfolded it, she said, "It's not my association. Not any more than it's yours." She scanned it, eyes working back and forth. One thing for sure, Angie had an ability to assimilate things quickly. "What about it?"

"What about it? You read it, right? According to that, they're planning to keep me from working at home."

An eye roll. "That's not so. They just don't want someone to have a home business with customers constantly coming and going. It decreases neighborhood security. You read the footnote, didn't you?" She handed the letter back.

I had taken in the footnote's rather massive presence, but hadn't bothered to read it. Okay, it did offer an out. But I would have to register my business with the neighborhood association and fill out a form that required certain information. The nature of my work. How many customers. The probability that they would come into the neighborhood. An approximation of my work volume. A paragraph of not more than 200 words describing my work schedule and an approximate dollar amount of business I would take in per year. "That's invasive," I said. "It's way too invasive. What jerk thought this up?"

The oven chimed, announcing the proper temperature. She placed the pan and batter in and turned, hands on hips. "I did."

I didn't know what to say, so I took in her glare without a word of response.

"According to the by-laws," she said, "the Board can prevent at-home work." I had my mouth open to agree with her overly-linear assessment, that this was my concern, too, but she held up a hand to stop me and continued. "Once they're created and filed with the state, they become like a law. Unless the Board changes them."

"We need to change that one, then. I won't put up with it"

Now her voice rose. "For Pete's sake, Warren, will you let me finish?"

I craned to see the countertop behind her. "Is there any coffee left?"

She turned, set a cup beside the pot, switched it back on. "So, with you in mind, I thought it wasn't fair, that you should have the opportunity to work at home without harassment from the current or any future Board. It could apply to someone else, too, you know. What if someone came down sick or had surgery and needed to work at home for a while?"

Appropriately humbled, I stopped her. "Sorry, I didn't know the whole story."

She had that look she used to wear when she was about to zing me good, but the doorbell saved me. Carly, a bottle of beer in hand, walked in. She must've noticed our grim expressions, because she stopped halfway to the kitchen. "Uh oh. You two lovebirds having a discussion? I'll come back, then."

Angie's manner transformed instantly. I'd never seen her emotional state change like that. Usually, her moods moved at the pace of a weather front in winter. Whenever we had a squabble like this one, she would remain pissed for days. Still, we hadn't seen Carly in a week, or Chris for that matter, so the interruption was a welcome one. "It's fine, just fine," said Angie, smiling and reaching for a Carly hug. "I'm making banana bread, and it'll be done in twenty minutes."

I chimed in; nothing like an exposed household spat camouflaged with neighborliness when a friend walks in. "It looks like you need another beer," I said to Carly. "Finish that one off and I'll get you another." I poured coffee for myself.

She gave me a what-in-the-world look and turned to Angie. "Just talked to Sadie. Madame President said to tell you your by-law amendment is approved. By acclamation."

Angie gave me a passing glance and said, "Really? By acclamation?"

"She didn't want to call a meeting for a formal vote. The others called her, and the lot of them approved it. Now. Since I'm here, I think I'll hang around for a piece of your banana bread. It smells delicious."

I bolted the lukewarm coffee and excused myself. It was Sunday, so I sought out Chris, and we took a walk down the hill, across Barberry's pasture, and up a ridge between us and Weaverville. A pretty day. The sky had spread its Carolina blue in a half-globe around us, except for one piece of cloud fluff and a couple dozen dots moving northward that I took to be Canadian geese. The trees were budding, alive with luminous, transparent greens. A soft breeze found us, fed us with its blend of coolness and warmth. I noticed a faint perfume-like scent. Wisteria, already? I looked around but saw none.

Chris chuckled. "Good medicine, springtime."

I glanced, saw his amused smile. "What?"

We walked a few more yards before he answered. "You were looking like you wanted to kill when we left the house," he said. "Now you're enraptured with springtime. What goes? Or rather, what was going on at home? You and Angie at it?"

Good old Chris. He's the only one I could talk to about my home life. Normally, an occasional spat between Angie and me was no one's business but ours, but her behavior — or rather, our skirmishes over issues she'd set in play — had me concerned. I had to talk to someone, but I didn't want him to think there was a long-haul conflict between Angie and me, so I said, "We were about to, but Carly came charging in and spoiled our fun."

He laughed at that, and we walked on.

"She said the whole neighborhood has been up in arms about my having an office here and working from home."

Chris has always been a fast walker; he already had a head start, and I had to yell to talk to him. He stopped and turned. A confused frown met me.

"Sounds like our neighbors," I went on, "are afraid my working at home will open the door to all sorts of intruders. We'll be crime infested. Property values will go down. That sort of thing. So she offered an amendment that'll require me to give the Board all sorts of work-related personal information."

His brow knotted. I continued. "There's this form I have to fill out and, I assume, if the Board doesn't like what they see from me, I might have to rent space somewhere in town to work."

As I spoke, he began retracing his steps toward me. He studied me for a moment. "Angie told you that?"

"Well, that's what I took from the letter the Board sent out. And from what she said."

"You have it wrong."

"Carly just brought over news that the Board approved a new amendment on the subject. Carly said it was approved without even taking a formal vote, so I figure the Board was thinking about doing a hatchet job on me."

He took another step forward, still studying me. Then he said, "Part of what you say is true, dude. What has me confused is, according to Carly, there's been no uproar in the neighborhood about your workplace. Everyone knows you work at home, and no one has ever had a problem with it. Angie came to the last Board meeting with the proposed amendment, you know, out of the blue, said she wanted to protect your right to work at home. The others told her it wasn't necessary, that your work wasn't the sort they might be concerned about. But she insisted the amendment be considered and voted on, because someone might object in the future and there should be a proactive way of dealing with it."

"Seriously?"

He grinned. "Yeah. You know those weekends and occasional times, like last week, when we're gone? We've been telling everyone who asks that we're on music gigs then, but it's only half true. Right before we moved in, Carly told me she wanted to check out a channeled being or some damn thing. So she went and came back all aglow with fervor to follow this imaginary guy. I smelled a rat, so I said I'd go with her next time."

I laughed. "What's his name?"

"I did go, and he doesn't have a name. He goes by a sign, an X inside a circle with some curly lines. But my suspicions were correct. The people involved with this discarnate being, some have given up promising professional careers and taken shit jobs to follow along, spend most of their paltry wages on trips to so-called power spots, for seminars, books, and such. The ones too invested in their careers to do that are pressured to pony up serious bucks to keep the whole thing afloat. Now the less affluent among them are impoverished, and the others are told if they want to keep tuning in, they have to bring the bucks." He paused for a moment, head down, kicking at a dirt clod. "That part ain't cheap."

"But you pointed out to Carly that it was bullshit, and she saw the light, right?"

"Not exactly. You're correct, I did have my say, but she's still all gooey-eyed over this thing."

Wow. This was hard to assimilate. We were walking again at this point, side by side, more leisurely than before, both of us silent. This didn't sound like the Carly I thought I knew, but I suppose everyone has something in their hip pocket they don't tell friends about. Too, Chris' flaky confession was adding to my confusion. "So why are you telling me this?"

We stopped again. Chris spun to face me. "Two reasons. First, I support my wife, no matter what she does.

But, second, if I weren't there with her, knowing her as I do, I'm sure she'd fold under pressure and commit to spending money we don't have." Another pause, this time longer, before he said, "You could say we're at odds over this, and you'd be right. But the fact that I'm there with her, quietly saying, "You should stop," when she gets out of control makes it manageable. Sort of." He chuckled at that, then his serious look returned. "You and Angie could have both been on the Board, you know, but when you said not no but hell no for yourself, she withdrew her nomination, even though she really wanted to be there, needed to in fact, from what Carly tells me. So she asked to be on the pool committee. She chose to do this thing for you behind your back, and because of that, you two have a lack of trust in one another."

He went on for a while about the channeled being's cult, saying that bleeding money from the followers was a power deal. Control their money, and you control them. As we finished our hike, I thought back to Angie's and my conversation over the letter. I now could see that the way I interpreted it had me thinking the worst. Still, her reply to my objections had done nothing to make me think differently. And I had no idea she wanted to be on the Board that badly.

What was going on between us? Was Chris right? Were we in a place where we didn't trust one another? We talked often, she and I, about all sorts of things. But the by-law change and her father's abuse — she must have found it difficult to talk to me about certain things, things she thought I wouldn't like or would disagree with. And I certainly hadn't done a good job of reading between the lines well enough to sense any of that. Too, was I failing to inform her properly when it came to things I was involved in? For instance, should I have talked to her more clearly about my interest in

Willard's work? Was that why she didn't like the guy?

Ten

$\mathcal{F}$ortunately, this was the week that the COVID-19 pandemic first appeared in media, and our mutual focus on its global gestation seemed to ease the friction between us. It began in China and that country was already reeling. SARS, MERS, Ebola, and a handful of other instant plagues had their perilous moments, too; eventually they were relegated to the medical dustbin, but this one seemed different. We began watching the pandemic reports on the evening news as the virus waltzed its way into Seattle, then Europe and New York City. Still, we both felt safe here in the mountains, and at first we were confident the city officials would tamp down its potential by ordering residents to procure and use gloves, masks, and lots of hand sanitizer. If they would do that, we could watch it pass us by. But that wasn't to be. Each night we watched reports on the virus' march across the country. We became obsessed with the reports, the nightly data as the count of those infected grew, the deaths growing at an equally rapid rate. One night, as the report began, Angie rose and headed for the bedroom.

I should have let her go quietly, but by this time I reacted to every little thing she did, every word she uttered, with concern if not guilt, and constantly questioned myself on whether I had done something that offended or threatened her. I was quickly discovering that despite our intended closeness, we really lived a world apart. I leaned back in my recliner so I could see down the hall, and just as she was about to disappear into the bedroom, I called out. "Hon, something the matter?"

For a moment, no answer came. Then she stepped back into the hall and said, "I can't watch that anymore. It's awful, all those people being infected and dying, and no one's doing a thing to head it off." She disappeared into the bedroom, slammed the door and, just like so many times before, the crying came.

I was unable to keep my mind on the TV, so in frustration I clicked it off and went for a walk. The air was cool and filled with the somnolent noises of night, a cricket here and there ahead of their annual chirp-fest, a lonesome owl and, very faintly, a few cars on the highway a half-mile through the woods. It was the first time I'd noticed that the noises sounded both distant and intimate, the result, I supposed, of the humid night air's ability to conduct sound. A full moon sat solemnly overhead, graced by a gossamer cloud just to its west.

I had no idea how far I walked, across the subdivision and into Barberry's pasture, then cut through some woods, and a short distance beyond on a dirt road I didn't know was there. I thought to stop, retrace my path and go to bed, but I was still a little anxious about Angie leaving me for bed at such an early hour. I kept going. The dirt road wound and then T-ed into a four-lane, and I knew where I was: I had walked some three or four miles in roundabout manner to Weaverville. Ah. The Waffle House was still open, and I had my wallet, so I strode across the all-but-empty four-lane.

"Hey!" a strong male voice called out. "Stop!"

I hadn't noticed the city police car in strip mall turn-in lane, a cop standing on his car's opposite side.

"Stay where you are," he said. He got into the car and crawled it toward me, the light atop it making loony circles about the dimly lit street. He got out, trotted to the car's far side, probably to protect himself from any late-night attack I might send his way. He motioned me over. "Let me see your ID," he said in that same commanding voice. "Slowly."

I pulled the driver's license from my wallet, set both on the car hood.

"Push it over here," he said.

I picked the license up, intending to hand it to him.

"No, set it down and do like I said. Push it over here, slowly."

I did.

He picked it up, shined a penlight on it, peered at me, then the license again.

"Hands on the hood."

"Really? You're kidding, right?"

His right hand went to his hip, where I assumed his weapon to be. I set my hands on the hood, beside my wallet. He strode around and patted me down from behind, set the license on my wallet.

"What're you doing out at this hour, Mr. Hardaway?"

I started to turn, facing him, but he shoved me back toward his cruiser.

"I said what're you doing out at this time of night?"

"I went for a walk," I said, "Got this far and saw the Waff—"

"From where?" he asked. "Where is Land Boulevard?"

"Off New Stock Road," I said. "Catawba Corners

Subdivision."

He glanced to my walking shoes. They were wet and a little muddy from my jaunt.

"Catawba Corners? That's some three miles from here."

"Sounds about right."

"Why were you taking a walk?"

He was beginning to piss me off, and I wanted to ask him why he didn't have anything better to do than hassle me, but that would probably have landed me in jail. "Like I said, just felt the urge."

"You didn't say that, Mr. Hardaway, but all right." He picked up my wallet, shoved the license into its vacant side pocket, thumbed through the money there. "You may go."

I turned, able to take him in for the first time, a stocky guy, not very tall. His chest was broad and deep. Oversized, muscular arms protruded from his short-sleeved uniform shirt bearing tats that looked like military-inspired art. "Gee, thanks, Officer…" I glanced at his nameplate. …Devons," I said it with as much sarcasm as I thought I could get away with, then pocketed my wallet, turned and strode toward the Waffle House.

Inside, I took a stool at the bar and let out a long breath, head in my hands.

"Hey, man, you okay?"

I looked up to see a not unattractive woman, probably in her mid-twenties, Gretchen, according to the name plate pinned to her Waffle House uniform. She absently brushed strawberry blonde hair from her forehead, hazel eyes roaming me, probably trying to figure out if I was trouble or not. "Yeah, I'm okay, was just out for a long walk, and a cop decided to hassle me."

"I saw. That was Darryl."

"Darryl? Darryl Devons? His parents favor alliteration?"

She frowned, clearly not getting that. "Darryl," she said, "he was my boyfriend."

"Was? Lucky you."

Again with the frown, not attuned to sarcasm, either. "You need a cup of coffee? Something to eat?"

I really hadn't come up with a compelling reason for being on a stool at the Waffle House. The cook was looking my way, trying his best to listen but maintaining a discreet pose. "Sure," I replied, "what the hell. Spinach omelet, bacon, extra crispy, and a waffle." I looked around the franchised greasy spoon, empty except for the three of us. "Think I'll take that first booth if you don't mind. Oh, and a cup of decaf."

She scribbled on a bill, but the cook was already working on my order. He had it ready in a flash, and the girl brought it over, him following. "I'm gonna catch a smoke," he said, smiling. "You can fill him in on Darryl." He disappeared out the back. She poured my coffee.

"So," I said, "sit and tell me about Darryl."

She poured a cup for herself, hobbled around the bar and collapsed into the seat across the table from me. "Thanks," she said. "I ain't got good shoes. My feet hurt."

"Darryl and you aren't together now, then?"

"Oh, hell no. He used to beat up on me."

I had to set my fork down at that. She was already beginning to wrinkle at the periphery of her eyes, either from poor nutrition or smoking. Or the stress of being around Darryl. She didn't look at all like Angie, but I began to superimpose her features on this girl. Gretchen carried the same wary expression Angie had adopted lately, and her tone of voice, which sounded as if she were slightly annoyed, was vaguely like Angie's as well.

"I'm sorry," I said. I sipped my coffee and started cutting the waffle into the little squares imprinted on it.

She gave me a timid smile. "It's okay. Me and Darryl are broke up now, like I said, and I took a peace warrant out on him." A quick glance to the picture window. Darryl's cruiser was nowhere in sight. "He kept calling up, said I couldn't break up with him. If it happened at all it would be him breaking off with me. What he does now is he patrols all over this street, and if he sees any guy he thinks might want to talk to me, he goes after him."

"The way he did with me?"

"Yeah." She said he had been in the army, went to Afghanistan, was indirectly involved in an unsanctioned civilian killing and given a general discharge. Then he went to work for a private contractor, was in Congo on the side of some warlord with lots of money. Came back broke. Gambling, she guessed, maybe prostitutes, looked for a police job, took the one here.

I pushed away my plate. "Look, if he's that bad, why didn't you take it to his superiors at the police department?"

Her eyes widened at the mention. "Oh, no, I could never do that. He'd kill me."

"Surely you don't mean that literally."

She glanced to the road beyond the Waffle house, seemed to shrink a little, and rattled out a dry cough. "I don't know. Maybe. I'm not sure. Say, you want more coffee?"

I said no, pulled a twenty out of my wallet, pushed it across the table. Then, and I don't know why I did it, I stood, bent, and kissed her forehead. She gave me a tentative smile, wriggled out of the booth, and hurried around the bar into the cook's and waitress' space beyond. She sighed, and her shoulders relaxed, as if being there afforded her a sense of protection.

It was two A.M. when I slipped into bed with Angie. She asked, drowsily, "Did you go somewhere?"

"Yeah. I took a walk. Went all the way to Weaverville. Had something to eat at the Waffle House."

That brought her fully awake. "With this corona thing going on? Why?" She sat up cross-legged facing me.

I moved to kiss her, but she dodged it, and my lips found only a cheek. "I'm sure it won't amount to much. Besides, no one here in the mountains has caught it."

Eleven

Another large envelope came the next day, from Willard. He had sent me a draft of more chapters about Hiram and the Catawba settlement for the *Smithsonian*. I wanted to sit and read the whole thing (there was a lull in tax preparation work now) but first I wanted to see if I could help Angie calm down about the virus.

Some were arguing that it came from weird animals people were eating. Conspiracy buffs claimed China had manufactured it in a lab and sent it to the States in revenge for our government tightening the screws on imports and intellectual theft. But come it did, to almost the whole world. It hadn't yet hit the country as hard as it eventually would, except in Washington State, a few cases coming though ports of entry on the east coast. At the time, I figured it was just another flu bug. No big deal. But Angie, as it turned out, had it in perspective, and she was freaking.

"Are you going to help?" she near-shrieked. She had everything that had entered the house over the last week on the breakfast bar, was wearing rubber gloves and wiping items with hot bleach water. She nodded toward the sink. "There's a pair of rubber gloves over there. Put them on, and see the bleachy water on the stove? Dip that big sponge in it and when it cools, wipe down the door handles, window latches, then the refrigerator door, anything you've touched since you came home last night. And when you've done that you need to —"

"Whoa, hon, don't you think you're a bit out of control here? The TV report says it's respiratory-based, it can't be transmitted by touch." I reached to hug her, but she squirmed away.

"And those clothes you had on when you went for your walk, did you put them in the washing machine?"

"C'mon, Angie, chill a bit, okay?"

She spun to face me, dropped a glass container, which shattered, spreading slimy, foaming liquid across our feet. She burst out crying, slumped into one of the kitchen chairs. I found a couple of old towels in the garage, handled the glass, wiped up the liquid, washed my hands, and reached out to take her in my arms. This time she didn't resist. We finished sanitizing the items on the table, and she retreated to a back room to set up a new plan for her next painting project.

But back to Willard's paper. Actually, it wasn't developing as much into a report as a book manuscript, some five hundred pages long, according to the page numbering, typed and double-spaced. Part of his *Smithsonian* commission was to include a series of drawings, an attached note revealed, which accompanied some of his artwork. Willard was indeed an artist; from Hiram's notebooks, he'd drawn two detailed head views of his forebear, made even more vivid through adept use of colored pencils. He had obtained recent aerial photos of the five ridges from an engineering company and superimposed on them his concept of the village. His dig downhill from our house, surrounded by Blakely-built homes, showed clearly, the Viking stone in the middle of it. Blakely had roped off the pit and, at Willard's insistence, built an inexpensive mini-park around it with a walkway to the eastern edge of the subdivision so the curious could, at some point, visit the site without much neighborhood interferance. At property's end, he had, again with Blakely's help, erected a large, semi-permanent sign depicting his view of the Catawba village layout, then covered it until his dig had been remediated.

The sign didn't show a rendering of the supposed and short-lived Viking settlement he'd found evidence of atop the much older fragments, but he'd included in his report an imagined drawing of it. All this atop the photos of our nearly completed development. In his summary, included in the last few pages, he wrote this:

"Cultures, towns, people, they come and go. Whole civilizations come into being, flourish and grow, and then they dwindle away and die. They leave their marks on the forests, the mountains, plains, and deserts, but the earth is the ultimate arbiter of life, and soon the scars cut into it by humanity are healed. Until the next encounter with human habitation. My work in archaeology has shown me a rather heretical thing: Whereas most life on the planet exists in symbiotic cooperation, far beyond the supposed instinctual abilities of flora and fauna, we humans are, for the most part, outliers. It's as though we're just visitors here, and not particularly benign ones where the planet is concerned. However, perhaps the more we discover about our origins on the planet, the more civilizations we uncover, the more we'll find out that humanity has a history of being an integral component of Earth's community of life. Still, I must write what comes from my era, my education, from the work I've been a party to. And those insights make me fear for the future of Planet Earth." Odd that he would get on his soapbox like that during such an innocent, non-political project. But what he wrote did make me think.

All has been quiet since last week's home sanitizing episode. Angie has calmed about the virus. I guess we're taking the epidemic in stride now; we're both back to our usual routines. I'm plugging away at a pair of audits that came in just yesterday, and Angie's down in the basement doing some macramé, a new hobby she's using as a respite from her other pursuits. I can't keep my mind on my work today; I keep thinking about Willard's excavations, his paper. I have it sitting on the top of my file cabinet, so I make myself a new pot of coffee and settle into my recliner to read some more of his imaginative work.

"Hannah," Hiram said to his Catawba wife, "see what all the noise is about out there." She stopped darning a pair of pants Hiram had managed to tear — a foot-long rip while escaping a buck deer he wounded. The animal struggled to his feet as Hiram approached and, full of adrenalin, charged, hooked a horn into his pants as Hiram scrambled up a low-lying oak. Hannah opened their cabin door to an October chill, pulled it shut and walked downhill to a young woman who had fallen to her knees in the tribal ceremonial area.

The woman wailed, a confluence of tears glistening as their stream cascaded down her cheeks. One hand gripped a flint knife. She had cut her buckskin gown and was slashing at an exposed breast. Hannah stopped an arm's length away. The woman raised her knife overhead, seemingly prepared to stab Hannah, who kicked it from her hand. That set the woman's wailing to a higher pitch.

"Stop it!" said Hannah in the Catawba dialect. "Why are you so upset, Ahyoka? No one has died. You have a good husband and three healthy children."

"No! My baby died in the night, and Waya is sick."

"Immokalee died? And your husband is sick? Come." The heftier Hannah lifted Ahyoka to her feet. "Let's make you a cup of tea and you can tell me what happened."

Ahyoka sniffed, nodded, and followed her to the cabin. Then words fell from her like autumn leaves. She told of a hound Waya had bartered an axe for, that the dog liked to chase raccoons and squirrels, that Waya loved the dog and wanted it at his feet when he slept. The baby had been born two months earlier, and during the past night he developed a rash and died.

Ahyoka rose to leave, her tea barely touched. Hannah gently settled her back onto a stool and asked, "And what of Waya?"

"He got the itch. Now I'm afraid he'll die, too."

Hannah turned to her husband. "Hiram, please see to Waya."

He sighed, stopped his braiding of a leather rope, rose, and lumbered downhill to Waya's shelter. Inside, the dead baby lay in Waya's arms as he moaned. Hiram felt of Waya's feet, then his hands and face. Warm. He had a rash similar to the one Ahyoka described that killed her baby. Hiram retreated, found a small wooden bucket, filled it from a cistern, tore the tail from his shirt, and mopped cool water onto Waya's forehead. Waya's moaning and writhing slowly stopped. He squeezed a portion of the water into Waya's mouth and left the shelter. The hound sat outside, scratching. Hiram bent to scratch the dog's back. A flea crawled onto his hand, and Hiram squashed it. He frowned, thinking, then rose, went inside, and untied Waya's tunic. Fleas. He killed as many as he could find in a cursory inspection, and unfolded the baby's blanket. More fleas. He returned to the cabin.

Ahyoka sat drinking her tea. She eyed Hiram, gave him a wary smile.

"What did you find?" asked Hannah.

"The baby is indeed…" He stopped for Ahyoka's reaction, received none. "…is gone."

Ahyoka began bawling again. Hannah stepped between the two. "Friend," she said to Ahyoka, "drink your tea, it'll make you feel better."

"No, I can't, it won't! My baby's dead and my husband will die."

"Perhaps not," said Hannah as she turned to Hiram. "Is he really sick?"

"Yes," said Hiram. "He has a fever. A bad one. He has fleas, and the baby has fleas all over her."

"Flea fever, then."

"Yes, I am sure of it. The dog has fleas as well."

Hannah tugged Ahyoka up. "You get back there, now, and you clean your husband. Cleanse him of all his fleas, you hear?"

Ahyoka nodded.

"I will clean the dog and bury the baby," said Hiram.

"No," said Hannah, "I will bury the baby. You kill the dog."

"'Tis not necessary to do the dog in, wife. I will cleanse it good."

For a moment she stared at him. "Do so. But she must be trained away from varmints or we will do this again. And do not bring fleas back here to my home."

One side of his mouth lifted into a smirk. "I built the

house. Final say about what is brought here belongs to both of us."

"Then take care of it in order that we may not have flea fever."

Hiram went for a walk, ears warm from the gentle chastising. On the way back, he stopped to check on Waya. The fever remained, but Ahyoka had wrapped him in a blanket, and he was eating a little stew Hannah had made.

"Have you handled the dog, husband?" asked Hannah upon her return from the burial.

"The bitch bit me," he said. "Then she ran to the woods."

She looked at his hand and laughed. "She has barely broken the skin. And you let her get away for that?"

"I'm hardly fond of a cur's teeth in my flesh."

Now Waya tried to laugh, but the itch began, and he moaned as he scratched.

"A word, husband," she said, and nodded toward the outside.

"I have seen this before," she said. "He will not live long."

Hiram glanced to the hut and shrugged. "He is fine by my accounting."

"Your accounting is as faulty as your dog handling. You must find the dog, and you must kill her. I tell you I have seen it. He will soon die." As she described the final stages of what she called flea fever, he nodded. He'd heard of it: typhus.

Hiram had seen it in person, too, but had been reluctant to tell Hannah of it. He didn't want to chase and kill the dog. What if he drew fleas to him from the bitch, came to ail in the same manner as Waya, and then die? No, it was best to let Hannah supervise Ahyoka's doings, and Hiram would let the dog run away.

Days passed. Waya grew heartier each day, but others in the village became sick. Babies died. Lactating mothers grew ill. The men were hit especially hard; more were growing ill by the day. Most had fevers and rashes. Others, not yet bedridden, stumbled about, confused and babbling.

One morning a group of men and women stood outside Hiram and Hannah's cabin and began to make noise. Some beat on a log section several of the men had carried up the hill. A few brought drums and began to pound them. Others simply yelled. Hiram appeared at the door with his rifle, and the noise intensified. One middle-aged man stepped forward and approached him.

"What is this about, Mohe?" asked Hiram.

"You must go," said Mohe. "The fever came because of you. You and your woman must go."

For a moment, Hiram didn't speak. "This is our home, Mohe."

"Only because our custom has been to accept others." As he spoke, his voice rose to a high pitch. Murmurs began. A few edged closer. One young man brandished a knife and began to yell. Mohe turned, raised a hand, and the younger man quieted. "You have brought the fever on us," Mohe said to Hiram, "and our people are dying. You must go."

More yelling and thrumming on the log.

Hiram handed his rifle to Hannah, who now blocked the cabin's doorway. "How many seasons ago was it that I came here?" he asked. "Some of you remember that day. Others of you are so young you only know of that day from the elders' stories. Have you forgotten? I brought food. I brought cooking wares and other items. And then the rains appeared. Do you remember the elk I shot? The drought ended and food once again became plentiful. Your corn flourished, as did your squash and beans, the herbs growing wild around us." He waved an arm to encompass the ridges and surrounding woods. The gathered group went silent. "I do not claim these good things happened because I came. Whether it was true or not, you believed it was so! You claimed I was a good sign, and you invited me to live here. I married one of your women. She took a white name; it was her decision to do so. Is that why you want us to leave, because I took a Catawba woman as wife? Together we have lived in harmony with you. You know this."

"You must go," Mohe repeated. The yelling and drumming began again.

Hiram turned to Hannah and spoke. She nodded.

"Mohe!" Hiram called out. "I will find Waya's hound and kill her and then we will leave. But you must do some things. Waya's dog has chased opossums and raccoons, and they gave her fleas. The fleas caused the fever. You must burn all your blankets, anything that carries the fleas. Burn them all. You must quit leaving food out that will feed the raccoons and opossums that carry these fleas. Some of you have hounds. You must keep them hobbled or tied to posts until this illness leaves the village. You must burn a wide arc around your shelters on each of the ridges to discourage flea-carrying animals from coming to you and your children. Do you understand?"

Throughout Hiram's speech, Mohe was arguing with the tribal shaman, the elder woman of the village. Now he turned to face Hiram. "Your presence here, it is what causes us to be sick. You must go."

"Will you do as I ask?"

"Go! You must be gone by nightfall."

The old woman neared Mohe and whispered, then shook a finger at him. He turned back to Hiram and in a quieter voice said, "Broken Wing has said we must allow you to remain until nightfall tomorrow. This will give you time to gather your things, and then you must go." He lumbered down the slope toward his shelter, and the people dispersed.

Hannah bent to the fireplace, stirred the coals. Flames leaped in a wild dance. She threw on a log segment, then another. Hiram watched her as she stirred and renewed the fire. "Hannah," he said. She didn't respond, so he repeated her name.

She turned, eyes glistening in the dim light of a lamp on the plank table between her and Hiram. "I do not wish to go," she said. "I will live with my brother. Our mother lives with him, she will say it is all right."

"No. The villagers will kill you if you stay. They will be forever angry with me, and they will take it out on you and your family. No, it is better that you leave with me. I will take you to the Big Sea, where people live in much larger villages, and I will find work there. We will save our money, and after some seasons have passed, I will return here. If the villagers' anger has passed, I will return for you, and we will use our money to bring more goods for their use. Food. Cloth. Rifles, lead, and powder. Cookware. Medicines. Please come with me. We will return, I promise."

"Hiram, will your people like me? Will they shun me and punish you for having a Catawba wife?"

"No. A few may try, but I won't allow it."

She skirted the table and ran to him. He buried his face in her hair, reveled in the warmth of her. For a long while, they held one another, said nothing, with only the crackling of the fire speaking.

I read this in fits and starts. I would stop, walk around, get a snack or a drink of water, check the coronavirus update on my phone, pay a bill or two, catch a moment of TV news, which was still nothing more than COVID-19 reports. By the time I reached this point in Willard's manuscript, it was nearing bedtime, Angie long since gone to bed. I resolved to read a couple more pages and then join her. Then I heard the bedroom door open, heard her padding softly down the hall to the bathroom. I was set to turn the page when she appeared in the door to the hallway. As things went with us, she would wait until she had my attention, then she'd come forward, smiling. This night she didn't smile. Instead, her eyes widened from their usual, sleepy, exotic beauty, her lips set in a taut line. She moved my feet aside, slipped onto my footstool.

"Warsie, I'm scared."

She rarely used the particular diminutive form of my name she'd dreamed up. I marked my place, set the manuscript on the floor beside the recliner, and said, "Scared? Scared of what?" I tousled her hair. "It's just the house settling in from the evening cooling…" My reply trailed off, because she now had my hands in hers, and they were trembling. Too, hers were usually warm as the blood pulsing through them, but now they were like icicles.

"Honey, what's the matter? There's nothing to be afraid of, not really —"

Crying now, she said, "Yes, there is, Warsie, this god-awful virus. I'm afraid I'll catch it. I don't want to die, not now, not like that."

She had been oblique in so many ways, indirect in our conversations, subtle, often too subtle for me to see her intent, her apprehensions about most everything that concerned her, but this was in my face. I realized I'd been too cavalier about this invisible mischief-maker and in being so, I hadn't honored her concerns about it. There had been no serious outbreaks nearby, though, I considered, so it couldn't really be the nearness of COVID that had her upset. I realized it was fear itself she was afraid of, and I could see no way to help rid her of what there no reason yet to fear. Still, her fear was real.

"I'm so sorry, Angie, I didn't realize this concerned you so much, but I —"

Her head snapped up, eyes narrowed. Instead of turning and walking away as she usually did in moments when I tried to negate her concerns, she said, "You didn't realize? Really? You didn't realize how concerned I was when we found out about the virus entering the country and then having everything out on the breakfast bar and cleaning like possessed people? Making you put the clothes you wore hiking into the washer with super-hot water to kill any virus on them? That didn't tip you off, even a little?"

Okay, that was sarcastic of her, but her point was crystalline in its clarity. We should have talked about it, and I know I'm making excuses here, but our ability to talk about really serious things had for a while been limited. I had long since given up on sitting down, nose to nose, and having one of those deep, understanding conversations that should be the basis of any viable relationship. But my emotional Achilles' heel is like that of most guys. I tweak the communication gene when something comes up, and if she responds, fine. But if she doesn't, and doesn't, and doesn't, then I let it marinate for a couple of days. If nothing more is said, I figure it's all a mood of the moment, and I go about my business, perhaps a little less willing to peer into the emotional depths with her next time.

"You're right, it should have told me something."

She had been leaning toward me, but now she came upright, hands jerked away from mine and jammed into her hips. "What's that supposed to mean? You've been thinking I was silly, that I'm just another addled female yelling wolf at the slightest thing?"

I never wanted to put it that baldly. I loved Angie, truly and deeply loved her, but I have to admit she nailed what I was reluctant to say aloud. I guess love has a way of registering bullshit in moments like that, shunting it aside and, hopefully, forgiving it at the same time. "Of course not," I lied, "I have never thought that."

Then the tears again. I reached for her hands, and she let me take them. "I'm sorry, Warsie, but I truly am scared. They say China is swamped with this damned virus and that it's coming this way. It's already shown up on both coasts and in Europe. Do you know how many people come into the U.S. from the Orient and Europe every day? It must be thousands. There's no treatment for the virus, and we don't have immunity to it." Now she was in emotional territory that was familiar to me — jaw set, grim determination beaming at me from those beautiful gray eyes of hers. A sigh, and she went on. "Look, I know I've been maybe a little extreme, but something feels wrong about this virus. Something really wrong." She gave my hands a little squeeze. "The virus will be here sooner or later if the experts are right, so can't we just practice? So that when it does hit us, we'll already be in the habit of doing the right things to protect ourselves?"

I couldn't help but smile. Why couldn't we talk like this more often? Why hadn't we done this many times before?

"All right, hon," I said, "we'll do that. We'll do exactly that. As soon as we find out what more we need to do to protect ourselves."

She leaned into me. We kissed, and she returned to bed.

Twelve

COVID did come to the Carolinas, and finally to Asheville. European travel through New York made it initially the epicenter of the Great Viral Death, and the virus came closer to home than we dared think. There was no testing for a long while, but then in May of the year, I had an appointment with my doctor, and he tested me. I sat in the cramped little room for a long while, not minding, really, because I had a book by a pilot who owns and flies a biplane, and his stories kept me spellbound.

Some forty minutes passed before Dr. Kirchheimer burst through the door, peering at me through a face shield and over his ventilating mask, strode to the computer terminal, and started banging away at the keyboard. His typing into some software or other left me to once more inspect the tiny room and its contents. He and his medical partner maintained a mom and pop-type practice, and the exam rooms were shabby and more than a little messy. I usually never touched the dog-eared *People Magazine* editions, fearing some disease lurked in the pages. But this day I lifted a half dozen of them away, and found a few copies of *Car and Driver*, an ancient copy of *LOOK*, that had come from who knows where, as well as some pharmaceutical pamphlets.

Dr. K sat on a stool that rotated, I in a ratty chair that was surely as uncomfortable as his thinly padded perch. The only thing in the room that wasn't shopworn was the exam table, which looked new. Neon lights shimmered and bleached the pale green walls. Strangely, the room contained no antiseptic smell, the way the other rooms did.

Finally, he hit a key with an artful flourish, spun on his stool, leaned onto the pale blue gown covering his knees, and said, "You have the virus, Mr. Hardaway."

The six words came through his mask muffled, and I was certain I hadn't heard him correctly. "I have the coronavirus, you say?"

"Yes." He walked his stool the few steps to me, pulled off his glove, and felt my forehead. "How do you feel?"

"I'm okay. Fine." Not totally true, but close enough so that I wasn't lying.

"Trouble breathing?"

"No. Well, maybe a little. I felt a little short-winded this morning during my walk. But only uphill. I rested for maybe a minute, then I went on. No problem."

He met my chopped sentences with grunts that, filtered through his mask, sounded a bit like Darth Vader. "Cough?"

I coughed.

A faint chuckle. "No, I meant have you had a cough. Dry throat, trouble breathing?"

"No, just a little from allergies."

He stuck a thermometer to my forehead. "Ninety-seven point two," he said. Then he slapped both knees, and said, "Your temp is the same as when you came in. So, unless you're not telling me the whole truth, you're asymptomatic."

I let out a long sigh and nodded.

"But you're not out of the woods just yet. Now that

you're confirmed, you may get it again. Does anyone in your family have the symptoms?"

Oh, man! Angie. I would have to tell her, of course, that I was going to self-quarantine. "No," I replied, "it's just me and my wife. No, no symptoms there." I wasn't totally sure about Angie, but neither of us had any reason to think the other was infected.

He gave me some advice on quarantining, and I left for home. I didn't want to walk into the house with the contagion of the century and announce myself, so I pulled into the Waffle House parking lot and called.

For a moment, a very long one, Angie didn't reply to my announcement.

"Look," I said, "I can move into a motel for a couple of weeks, see how this shakes out."

That didn't prompt an immediate response, either. Finally, she said, "No, I want you home. Let's put you in the spare room, okay? We'll have to figure out how we can share the bathroom, but we'll make it work."

That brought tears to my eyes. She could just as easily have agreed to have me out of the house, and now we'd have a lot to figure out and be cautious in the doing. She was risking her life to keep me at home.

"Can you give me an hour to get some things moved into the spare room?" she asked.

I said of course, I would stop by the Waffle House, which seemed to have remained open at all costs, for a cup of coffee and a sandwich. Angie had bought a pack of masks at CVS, and I had maybe a dozen in my Jeep, so I put one on and went in. A couple of coffee drinkers sat at the bar, an old couple was eating a late lunch in a booth. I was about to walk out when the cook from that late-night sojourn I made came in. He looked blankly at me at first, then in a moment of recognition, he came over, smiling.

"Say, you're the guy Darryl Devons was hassling that night, ain't you? I could tell who you was, even with that mask on."

"That's me," I replied, "unless he's a serial hassler, in which case I could be any one of them." That put a quizzical look on his face, so I added, "But, yes, I came in late one night after the cop put me through a midnight search. I had coffee and talked with your waitress, Gretchen, for a few minutes."

Something dawned on him, and he backed away a couple of steps. "You ain't got the virus, do you?"

"I'm afraid so. I'm asymptomatic, so hopefully I won't get sick."

"That's what I was afraid of. I don't know if you heard or not, but Gretchen got the virus, too."

That floored me, because what was dawning on him was now all too apparent. Gretchen had given me the coronavirus. "I'm so sorry," I replied. "Do you know how she's doing?"

He rubbed his hands together, said, "It ain't looking too good, according to her mama. She lives with her mama, y'know, and she told us Gretchen's in a bad way."

"She's been hospitalized, then."

"Yessir, that's what her mama said. What with her smoking and all, it don't look like she's gonna make it."

"She told me she'd been dating that cop. Do you know if he has the virus?"

The skin around his eyes wrinkled a bit, telling me there was a grin beneath the mask. "Just between you, me, and the gatepost, I wouldn't mind if he did get it, but no, sir, he's healthy as a racehorse, best I and tell."

An elderly couple shuffled in, showing downcast looks. The wife was wiping tears away.

"Something wrong?" asked the cook.

The old man nodded. "We just heard that your Gretchen died. It's such a shame. She was so young."

The cook hurried around the counter and hugged them both. Then he turned my way, tears glowing. "She was such a good-hearted young'un."

"Yeah," I said, "I got that feeling."

He poured me a cup of coffee and cut a piece of pecan pie. I took them without a word. Finished, I headed for the cash register, but he waved me off. "It's on the house," he said. I shook my head, left a folded five on the counter. He pocketed it, and his smile wrinkled his mask, a red and black handkerchief. "You keep your loved ones safe, okay? Don't need no one else getting that virus."

It was a six or seven-minute drive home from there. I had to decide what more to tell Angie when I got there. I went the long way around, through downtown Weaverville. I felt I needed more time than that to orchestrate my virus tale, I pulled into a parking space at Lake Louise, sat a few minutes, and drove to Weaverville, parked in the city lot across from the bakery. Angie was being so understanding about my having COVID, but it hadn't come up regarding where I'd caught it. Maybe it wouldn't. But no, it would eventually. Maybe not today, but at some moment in the future when I was least expecting it, Angie would ask. What should I say? That I don't know? I hadn't been out much lately, given client taxes and other work I had, so where else would I have been infected?

I turned on the radio, closed my eyes, and listened to a talk show, tried to forget the virus. No, that wouldn't do. I needed to get home, talk to Angie, tell her…something. It seemed like only a few seconds before I was pulling into the garage. I knew the answer, had known it the whole time. I had to tell the truth. Maybe not the entire truth but enough to satisfy Angie and my swollen, thumping conscience. The door between the garage and hallway opened, silhouetting her. She stayed some ten feet from me as I entered the house. We stopped in the kitchen, she against the cabinet next to the sink, I in the doorway.

"Warren, how did you contract COVID?"

Well, there we were. No pregnant pause, no week of dread wondering if and when the subject would come up. Okay, Warren, out with it, don't try to hide from it, just tell it. "Yeah, I was thinking about that on the way home. The night waitress at the Waffle House, Gretchen, she died from it today. I think that's where I got it."

For a moment Angie said nothing. She just stared past me, into some faraway place.

"You okay, hon? You look like you've seen a ghost."

She just stood there, not seeming angry or hurt, just a perplexed look on her face. "You got it from a waitress? What does that mean?"

"You remember that night I took a late walk and ended up at the Waffle House? When the cop hassled me? She saw it happen, and when I did go in, she sat down with me for a few minutes, told me what a creep the guy was." There. It was done. The story was out, and this would be the end of it.

She turned to the sink, washed her hands, and when she turned back, that winsome smile of hers had made an appearance. "Did you eat anything? Can I fix you something?"

"I had coffee. A small piece of pie."

"A BLT, then?"

"Yeah, that sounds great."

While she toasted the bread and cooked the bacon, we talked of other things, the meaningless moments that make up a married home life. Some of the shrubs had been burned by frost during the winter, and they needed to be pruned. The toilet was making gurgling sounds, and it seemed to be running occasionally when no one had been in there in a while. Daylight through the kitchen window had bleached the new linoleum floor. She'd felt flush earlier in the day, took her temperature and had been sneezing. Her temp was only a half degree above normal and the sneezing had stopped. We both agreed the temp wasn't an issue and the sneezing had been set off by early pollinating plants.

I took a Coke from the fridge, sat at my usual place at the breakfast bar, and she set the sandwich before me. The lettuce was crisp and cool, the thick tomato slice juicy, and I near-inhaled the sandwich. She laughed softly as I licked the mayo off my fingers.

"You don't want another, do you?" Her little laugh was infectious, and I laughed, too.

"No, this will do."

"So did this Gretchen cough on you? Is that how you got the virus?"

I set my Coke down at that. "I told you, hon, she sat down across from me that night. We talked for a few minutes, and I left."

"She didn't cough or sneeze?"

"No, not that I remember."

"You didn't touch her?"

"No, not really. She was telling me about living with her mother and how that cop had been physically abusive, so when I got up to leave, I gave her a little peck on the forehead."

Her eyes narrowed. "You kissed her?"

Now why did I tell her that? It wasn't necessary, I still believe that, but then I had promised not to hide anything from her. "A little peck on the forehead? Do you think that was how I got the virus? From that little peck?"

"Warren, were you having an affair with her?"

Okay, at this point I had to hold my temper. I understood her concern, but she should have known I would never do that. I've never loved anyone else the way I loved Angie, and I can't imagine having an extramarital affair with anyone, even now. It's just not in my makeup. I took a deep breath and said, "No, of course not."

"That's it, then? That's all you have to say for yourself?"

"What's that mean? I told you what happened and why. It was an accident that the cop showed up to give me a hard time, and then it was a coincidence, I guess, that she sat down at my booth and told me about her ex and her family life, and that little peck was just an innocent response to show the poor girl a little sympathetic affection. That's it."

A long sigh. "All right. Your things are in the guest room. I moved the small TV in there for you, too."

I knew better than to say more, so I changed clothes and took in what she had done. My clothes were neatly arranged, the TV set at just the right place for me to lie in bed and watch late night shows. She had moved my laptop and my most recent work projects to the small secretary we kept in there for guests. She'd even moved the mini-fridge in from the garage and stocked it with snacks, drinks, and makings for sandwiches. All in an hour. God, I loved that woman.

Thirteen

It didn't take long for word to get out that I had COVID. I think it was Carly who Angie first told. It would have been, of course, and it would have been Carly who spread the news. She's as adept as CNN about getting news out. From what Angie told me, most of the neighbors were sympathetic, although the story grew as it circulated. One couple thought I was dying, that Angie wouldn't let me go to the hospital for fear of infecting those there.

Another couple, one of the neighborhood originals, sent us threatening e-mails. We were, they declared, dangerous to the health and welfare of the rest of the neighborhood, and they demanded we move. We wrote them off as kooks and didn't respond. Then they sent us an ultimatum: if we didn't move, they would take us out. "What do you suppose that means?" Angie asked. I didn't know for sure what they had in mind. It could have meant they would physically remove us from the house and neighborhood. Or it could mean the obvious — they would kill us.

One morning around five-thirty A.M., I woke to Angie crying and banging on the bedroom door. "Warren!" she wailed, "wake up, honey, please. We're under attack!"

I go into a deep state of unconsciousness when I'm

asleep, and it took her a couple of minutes to roust me out. For some reason, I'd locked the bedroom door, as if I were in a hotel room, and it took me a moment to fumble the door lock open. Still crying, she threw her arms around me, buried her flushed, overly-warm face in my shoulder. It was okay, though, for her to do that, I thought; I was one day from finishing my quarantine period.

"Honey, someone's shooting at us," she said between sobs.

"Shooting? What do you mean? Someone's firing guns out front?"

Bleary-eyed, she shook her head. "No, into the house."

"Are you hurt? Is anything damaged?"

"Th–they shot out the living room window. You didn't hear it?"

As we headed for the living room to inspect the damage, I said, "Did you call the cops?"

"They'll be here in a minute."

Maybe three minutes elapsed before an oscillating light sent its tentacles through the living room. I went outside to meet the policeman. The silhouetted officer's bulky shoulders seemed familiar. He stood behind the open cruiser door, shining a flashlight on me. "Stop right there," he called out when I was maybe fifteen feet away, "and turn around."

The order had a familiar, annoying ring. "Are you kidding me?" I called out.

"That's what I said, now turn around, and get your hands up."

It was Devons, the cop who had rousted me at the Waffle House. I turned around, hands high. His footsteps clumped closer, then those beefy hands patted me down. A ridiculous effort; I was in sleeping shorts and a tee shirt. "All right," he said, "so why am I here?"

I lowered my hands and turned around. "Someone shot through our house. It must've been high-powered, because the bullet went through the plate glass window and through the back wall."

"I need to see it," he said.

The outside floods came on, Angie standing in the doorway wearing a bathrobe.

Devons tensed, as if ready for action, and said, "Who's that? Who turned on the lights?"

For a cop, he didn't seem very swift on the uptake. "That's my wife. She's the one who heard the shot, and she turned on the lights."

"Who else is in the house?"

"No one else, just the two of us."

"All right, I'm going in," he said. "I'm following you."

He shoved me up the steps and in. Angie had the lights on throughout, and Devons edged down the hall, peering into rooms.

"The living room's the other way," I said, but he ignored me, looked into every room, plus the garage. Angie had made a pot of coffee, already sipping a cup, so I poured myself one, and we waited.

He ended his walk-through in the kitchen. "You have a guest that you didn't mention?"

"Warren sleeps in the guest room," said Angie.

Devons' dour expression transformed into a faintly amused smile. "Is that right."

"I have the coronavirus," I said, "so we're sleeping apart for two weeks."

The smile fell from Devons' face and he backed away. "So you're the one who gave Gretchen the virus."

"No," I said, unable to look Angie in the eye, "I'm pretty sure it was the other way around. Say, are you going to look in the living room at the damage the bullet caused?"

He didn't respond; instead, he left the house and peered up at the bullet hole in the living room window, smiled, and returned to his car. I followed a few steps behind. The sun's first glow was beginning to swell on the eastern horizon. He opened the driver's side door and moved to its opposite side, the door between us. "Something you want?" he said.

"Going to get the paper." It lay near one of his rear wheels, and as I bent to pick it up, I noticed a rifle on his back seat with what appeared to be one of those long-range telescopes on it. I don't know if it was or not — I'm innocent regarding such things — but it could have been a military sniper rifle. "Look, Devons," I said, "I had nothing to do with Gretchen contracting the virus. I don't want trouble with you."

"Then stay out of my way," he replied. He said he'd file a report and he left.

"What was that about?" Angie asked as I walked in, shut and locked the door.

"You heard him. He blames me for Gretchen's death."

She returned to her coffee and began pancakes for an early breakfast.

Two days later, we woke to find our front stoop festooned in yellow police tape, with a sign on our mailbox that read: QUARANTINED.

Angie wrung her hands and asked me, "Why is this happening, Warren?"

I suspected this was Devons' handiwork, but I wasn't going to let his name come up again. "The virus has a lot of people scared, including some of our neighbors. We'll have to stick even closer to home, I guess."

"No," she said. "We won't. We're going to do whatever the hell we want." She was shaking a finger in my face, her breathing rapid, in panic mode, I thought. "We'll wear one of those goddamned masks, and we'll do exactly what we want to do." Now her eyes sparkled with excitement. Perhaps her saying all this was an attempt to believe it herself, to summon the nerve to flip off the neighbors, to not be intimidated by the sour reaction many around us were having to my COVID. "You're with me on this, aren't you?" she asked.

Laugher poured from me. My viral infection had made me feel less than human, inferior to all who knew me, all who sought to come in contact with me. This ballsy pose of hers so soon after our being shot at and pushed around by Devons was the catharsis we both needed. "Damn right I am, hon. We'll be safe, but we won't be sorry."

Then she passed out in my arms.

The EMS people came quickly. By the time they arrived, she was having trouble breathing, and the oxygen they gave her wasn't helping. She had a fever, and it had climbed into the danger zone. The head EMT announced that Angie had COVID-19. Two of them brought in a gurney; they hustled her into their vehicle and drove off. Numb, I stood in the doorway for maybe five minutes after they left. I had brought the virus into our home and given it to the person I loved most in the world. By the time I arrived at the emergency entrance to Mission Hospital and announced myself though my mask, she was being triaged. A nurse appeared in seconds with a swab, stuck it into my right nostril, worked it around, and headed to a lab room. She returned in gear that looked like a Hazmat suit, took my temperature, and asked me a host of questions. Then:

"Have you had the coronavirus, Mr. Hardaway?"

"Yeah. I was tested a few days ago."

Her eyes narrowed. "You knew? And you exposed your wife to it?"

Really? I'm being accused of carelessness with this virus? I told her the whole thing: I had been exposed to it myself, the other person didn't know she had it, and I didn't know I had it, since I was asymptomatic. I was tested at my doctor's office on a normal visit, I told her, called my wife on the way back, and she arranged for me to be quarantined in our home for the two-week period. That period was almost over when she passed out and I called EMS.

That brought more questions, one of which took us to Gretchen.

"Gretchen Applebaum, yes, I remember her. She died some time ago," said the nurse. "You didn't communicate with one another about the virus?"

"No."

A doctor had approached and was listening. "Why not?" he asked.

"As I was just telling your nurse, I didn't know she had it, I didn't know she'd given it to me, and by the time I found out I had it and she had given it to me, she was dead." My voice had risen as I spoke, and heads were turning in the emergency waiting room.

The nurse seemed prepared to advance her accusations a few steps further, but the doctor said, "All right, all right, calm down. Unfortunately, this isn't out of the ordinary, given what we currently know about the disease. Were you able to self-quarantine at home?"

"I have one day left. I want to see my wife."

"I'm sorry, sir, but that's not possible. She's in pretty

bad shape, and our protocol —"

"I don't give a damn about your protocol," I shouted. "I want to see my wife. Now!"

He sighed, motioned for me to follow, and led me to a ward populated with a dozen beds, an overflow area for COVID, he informed me. Only one, Angie's, was occupied. A pair of nurses were prepping her for IV and oxygen. The doctor asked them about Angie's breathing. One shook her head. He turned to me, said, "It looks like she'll be on a ventilator as soon as we can get one brought up."

I took a step toward her. The doctor grabbed at my arm, missed, and before he could recover, I was at Angie's side. Her eyes were closed, her face a pale blue, lips puffy. I bent to her ear. "I'm so sorry, honey, I didn't know I was sick, and you didn't know you were sick. "I'm so very sorry. Get well, honey, and I'll see you soon."

I think I noticed a minuscule nod, and she definitely smiled as I spoke. The doctor worked his way between us, gently pushed me toward the door.

Fourteen

*T*wo weeks later, Angie was still on a ventilator. Since the hospital still had fewer COVID patients than they eventually would, the nurses didn't yet have their hands full. So every day I called, asked for the head nurse on that floor. I didn't manage to get her to the phone many days, but when I did, I remained in a state of acute anxiety, fearing she would report that Angie's condition was worsening. But no, for the first week, and then the second, she remained stable, although still having extreme difficulties breathing. I wanted to see her, to hold her hand, to whisper, just to let her hear the sound of my voice. And every day I tried to cajole the management there into allowing me to do just that. Finally, the nurses began to be too busy to do any emotional hand-holding with me and I lost track of Angie's condition.

I tried to work, but I was making careless mistakes with the numbers and data. Fatigued with worry, I began to nap a lot. When awake, I paced compulsively, found myself too often in front of the TV. Such lousy work habits meant writing emails to my clients, telling them my wife had the virus, was in critical condition, and I was preoccupied with her health. If they wanted to shift their tax preparations to another firm, I would be glad to recommend someone. It was both gratifying and burdensome that they stuck with me. I promised if any problems arose with my work, I would indemnify them as best I could.

Deep into that second week, the phone rang. Caller ID informed me it was Carly.

"Warren, hi," she said almost in a whisper. "Look, I was wondering how Angie's doing."

"To be honest," I said, "I don't know very much. The nurses…" I heard Chris's voice in the background calling out to her.

"I need to go," she whispered, "I'll call you back in a few." An abrupt hang up.

Odd, I thought, but I blew it off, tried to work, but couldn't. All I could think about was Angie. Whenever I managed to contact someone there who had a minute, they would only give me a very broad-brush view of Angie's care. It amounted to telling me they were servicing her ventilator, or were in the process of feeding her intravenously, or had just received a bloodwork panel and everything seemed fine. I really had no feel for her overall progress.

An hour later, Carly called again, and I resumed where I left off with what I knew of Angie's situation. She listened, asked me a few specific questions I couldn't answer. Then she said, "Chris will be back in a few minutes, so I just wanted to call. Give Angie my love, will you?"

She was talking to me on the sly? She didn't want Chris to know she was talking to me? Were they having marital problems, Chris didn't want her to talk to and about their best friends in the neighborhood? Ordinarily, I wouldn't have thought much of the innuendo. In their own way, Carly and Chris were as quirky and mercurial as Angie and I sometimes were. During normal weeks and months, when one of them had said or done something out of the box (and I couldn't help but remember his story about Carly's dalliance with a discarnate entity), I would ask Chris what was going on with them, he'd tell me, it'd usually be nothing, and we'd laugh about it.

"Wait, Carly, don't hang up yet," I said. "What's going on? You don't want Chris to know you're calling?"

A pause before she said, "I guess you and Chris haven't talked in a while."

"No, I thought that was a little odd, but maybe he's been busy, and then there's my being quarantined —"

She coughed, cleared her throat. "All right, I guess you have a right to know. Chris doesn't want anything to do with you."

Now my concern was morphing into annoyance. "Doesn't want anything to do with me? Why? What does that mean?"

Another pause. "I'm sorry, Warren, but you have to understand what's going on in the neighborhood."

"What're you talking about, Carly? Are you saying the neighborhood is shutting us off because of the virus?"

"Well, yes, that's pretty much it, I guess, and again I'm so sorry this is happening. But someone said you were having an affair with that girl at the Waffle House, and you gave her the virus, and then you gave it to Angie and, well, that girl died and Angie may, too."

"Wow, Carly, that's all bullshit, and I would have thought you and Chris would recognize it as such."

A sob. "I don't, I mean, I really don't want to believe anything like that, but everyone knows about it."

Now I began shouting. "Everyone knows what, Carly? The only thing you've said that's true is I gave Angie the virus, and that was only because I didn't know I had it. Even the doctor said it's not my fault —"

"I need to go, Warren," she said, whispering, "Chris just drove up." The phone went dead.

Where in the world would Carly and Chris and, for that matter, the whole neighborhood, get the idea that I was having an affair? That I had given Gretchen the virus? And from the sound of it, that I'd given Angie the virus deliberately? Is everyone that frightened of this virus? Would they make stuff up about us, make up lies about me because they fear the virus?

I guess there really is a morbid, fear-based trait people have that makes them react to diseases and other unfortunate situations by demonizing those caught up in those circumstances. Well, Angie was right; I couldn't, wouldn't, knuckle under to neighborhood drama. I'd find out what's behind these rumors. But first I wanted to let Chris know that what he'd been hearing was wrong. We'd never been though any contentious moments over the time we lived there, and we trusted one another. He'll listen to me, I determined, even if no one else will.

I grabbed my phone and punched in the number. He didn't answer, so I called again. This time he did answer. I imagine Carly demanded it of him.

"Yeah?" His gruff tone told me Carly was right; he didn't want to talk to me.

"Look, I'm certainly not spoiling for a fight," I said, "but you and I have always been straight-up with one another, so I want to tell you, I didn't have an affair with Gretchen."

"Who?"

"The Waffle house waitress, the one who died of coronavirus." I waited for a response, but nothing came.

"There's this rumor going around that I was having an affair with her, that I had the virus, I gave it to her, and then I purposefully gave it to Angie."

"And you're saying you didn't?"

"Of course I'm saying that. Don't you know I wouldn't have an affair, that I love Angie? I wouldn't give her this virus. I just wouldn't."

"But you did. And people do things like that all the time. You and Angie were having some problems, or don't you remember?"

"Come on, Chris! Sure, I didn't understand some of Angie's motivations for things she did, but if I were the kind to start offing women indiscriminately, we would never have become friends in the first place."

"Like I said, people do things."

I could see I was getting nowhere. "All right, if you want to believe this, then I'm sorry you do. I called to tell you it isn't true. I just wish I could find the root of this thing and stop it."

"It was in the police report," Chris said. "Apparently you told all this to a cop."

Ah. I get it now. Devons. He was jealous, certain in his deranged mind that I was trying to steal his ex-girl. I would have to straighten this out somehow, but I didn't want Devons shooting out another window. Or worse. "No, I didn't tell any such thing to the cop. Darryl Devons is his name, and he's the one who shot out our living room window."

"Cops don't do that," he said in a patronizing voice. "You're looking for a scapegoat, something or someone to blame for your screw ups. And let me say this, too. I remember how quickly you rushed into thinking Angie was messing with you about your working at home, for reasons you couldn't come up with."

"I know that, Chris. We weren't talking a lot. It was difficult, even before Angie got sick. Angie didn't explain her actions, she didn't consult with me."

"And you thought the worst about her," he persisted. "Didn't you?"

"I did. Look, I guess I'll just have to prove things to you."

He laughed, full of sarcastic overtones. "I don't believe you can, Warren."

So now the gauntlet was on the ground, somewhere between their house and ours. It hurt for a good friend not to consider giving me the benefit of the doubt. I stomped my way into the garage and left, having no plan whatsoever concerning how to prove something that probably couldn't be proven. Chris would smile and tell Carly that I didn't have the strength of character to admit the police report was correct. I decided to drive to county police headquarters.

There, I announced myself, and asked, as politely as I could manage, to talk to someone about the police report. The cop at the desk looked me over, as if trying to figure out if I was trouble or not. He took enough information to home in on the report I was there about. An aha gleamed in his eyes, and he nodded. "What about it, sir?" he asked.

"I didn't know about the report, and if what I'm being told is true, it contains some erroneous information."

He didn't respond for what must have been a full minute. Then he pressed a button on his phone. "There's a guy out here who wants to talk with you about Devons."

That wasn't exactly what I'd asked for, but it would do. The captain, a tall, amiable fellow, appeared, ushered me into his office and closed the door behind me. I told him who

I was, and he directed me to a chair in front of his desk. He let me drone on for a couple of minutes about Devons and the Waffle House drama, then he stopped me.

"Officer Devons was let go this morning," he said. That left me with my mouth open but mute, so he continued. "I'm not at liberty to discuss the details, but I have read his report about the Waffle House episode and his visit to your home. There will be an investigation, so don't worry about either incident. That's all I can tell you at this time."

Fifteen

*T*urns out that Devons, despite his willingness to write long reports about every incident, important and inconsequential, wasn't very good at writing them. He tended to overly dramatize incidents and mix fact with opinion. It quickly got around town, I found out, that if you had an encounter with Officer Darryl Devons, you'd better ask for the police report. So it didn't take many months for the police department to start monitoring his reports, and then turn them over to their psychologist for evaluation.

Then my incident at the Waffle House occurred. The neighbors hadn't heard of his reputation; when still-unknown-to-me ones managed to access the report, they were unaware of the initial version, kept in a dead file unavailable to the public, which was a sketchy but step-by-step of what happened. Only the addendum was available by that time. That little gem accused me of killing Gretchen with my COVID out of jealousy. My thinking, according to Devons, was that I couldn't stand the fact that she'd once been his lover, that she wanted him back, so I killed her. He wrote further that he expected me to kill myself over her death. That was the report putting Devons into counseling, and much came of it. When he learned the force was going to dismiss him for being too mentally off-beam to pursue police work, he threatened to kill the captain, the chief of police, and finally himself. The local force called in the state bureau of investigation, and when they and various medical people showed up at his apartment to escort him to a mental care facility, they discovered he had skipped town.

So with Devons gone, and with my lawyer's help, I managed to copy the counselor's letter to the police force, which didn't say much other than Devons was sick and that his reports, particularly the addenda he usually tacked on, tended to be bogus. On the pretext of being concerned with Chris's opinion of me, I told Carly all this, even sent her a scanned copy of the letter, knowing she would broadcast its contents across the neighborhood. I didn't receive any apologies from the neighbors, nor from Chris, and didn't expect any, but a nurse told me Angie began receiving an occasional flower bouquet and get-well card at the hospital.

Her condition still wasn't improving. They took her off the ventilator, then had to put her back on. Her vitals tanked, and then she slipped into a coma-like state. When that happened, I could no longer stay away. I made an appearance at the hospital and demanded to see the doctor in charge of the coronavirus ward. It took most of that day, but he did show, clad head to toe in personal protective gear.

He stopped a few feet away. "I'm Dr. Masood, Mr. Hardaway," he began. "I don't know what more I can tell you about your wife's situation, except that she's doing as well as can be under the circumstances —"

"As well as can be? You let her slip into a coma, for crying out loud."

"Unfortunately, it's not out of the ordinary with this virus."

When I get as steamed as I was talking to him, I have an urge to pace. I realized I couldn't do that if I was going to be effective in getting any information from him (eye contact, and all that), so I rocked back and forth where I stood as I bellowed at him.

"You must calm down, sir," Masood said. "We must discuss this calmly."

"All right," I said, trying to do just that. "Then calmly tell me what's going on with my wife. What's changed? Why is she in a coma?"

I guess he decided to compensate for his diminutive stature by displaying a little anger of his own. "It's not a coma," he yelled back at me. At least he tried to, but his voice came out, not booming, but squeaky and nervous. "It's not a coma, Mr. Hardaway," he repeated, "you must understand this. It's a coma-like state."

"What, are you a politician? What the hell's the difference?"

He kept looking at my feet, which, I realized, were still shuffling. "We are having to learn as we go with this virus, Mr. Hardaway. All I can tell you at this time is that it's not out of the ordinary."

I wanted to tell him I didn't give a damn about what was ordinary or not, but I choked that back, took a deep breath, and said, "Okay. What caused it?"

"I can only hazard an opinion. When patients have been on a ventilator long enough, we realize that, even with such technology, the patients haven't been getting enough oxygen. Coupled with that, we can only feed them a small amount, and that goes into a feeding tube. So it's not surprising that the body copes by going into a simulated coma."

This wasn't sounding good. Was he trying obliquely to

tell me Angie was dying? So I asked.

"Once again, we don't have enough data to say that."

"But that's what you're thinking, isn't it?"

"A few patients seem to get through this stage, Mr. Hardaway. We don't know why they do, and we don't know why others don't."

This was exhausting me. I couldn't go on demanding details he was either unwilling or unable to give me. I thanked him, begged him to tell me personally when there was a change in Angie's condition one way or the other. But he didn't promise anything of the sort; he simply nodded and turned away.

On the way home, I finally realized how bad off Angie was. She'd been on a ventilator for over two weeks. I didn't know what that looked like, or felt like, but I knew that under the circumstances, she was in bad shape. It occurred for the very first time that I really might lose her. I pulled off the Interstate, found a grocery parking lot, and cried until the tears quit coming. At home I realized I no longer knew what she looked like. I dug out a photo album and stared at her face in the snaps. I went to the bedroom, sniffed her pillow. Then I pulled back. I couldn't do this to myself. The Masood fellow hadn't said she was dying. She might very well survive, come home, and live a long life. I had to divert my attention until something shook out. I picked up Willard's manuscript and began reading, in fits and starts, as I could manage. I had left off at the place where Hiram and his Catawba wife, Hannah, were leaving the village:

The couple didn't need to take much with them, just some foodstuffs, clothes, a few pots and pans, some doeskins to barter, two rifles, a pistol, ball and powder, and a pair each of deerskin boots Hannah had made. Hiram packed these on their mule, Abraham, and they began their long trek to the east. Hiram had aged since arriving in the mountains, and the trip proved arduous for him.

They followed the Broad River for a while, traveling through the difficult mountain terrain. The couple camped for a week in the foothills of what is now South Carolina so Hiram could regain his strength. On the third day there, he shot a young doe, dressed and quartered it, and Hannah began the process of curing the hide. Rejuvenated by their rest, fresh meat, berries, herbs, and clear, cold water in these beginnings of the lush meadowlands, they packed Abraham once more and, after another week, turned eastward. The vast meadowlands provided more food. They bartered the venison and doeskin for game birds, squash, and beans within a Native American encampment. Hiram pushed hard after that, and six weeks later they arrived at the mouth of the Cape Fear River and the village that is now Wilmington. Few structures stood there then: a small dock, a log warehouse for goods barged in from British and French merchant ships, a tavern, a small log building that served as a store, and a half dozen lodges occupied by an encampment of Waccamaw Indians.

For a month, they took up lodging in first one Waccamaw lodge then another. Hiram took work adding rooms onto the tavern. The money was good and, befriended by the Waccamaws, he and Hannah were able to save almost all he made there. Then bad luck found them.

Hiram and a free black man were working near the settlement cutting down pines. They left them on the ground to cure for a few weeks before using Abraham to drag them to the tavern addition. One day, as they felled a huge one, the tree fell the wrong way. Hiram dropped his axe and backed away, tripping over a previously fallen pine. The tree they had just cut glanced across his right leg as it came down, breaking the tibia. The tree bounced and came to rest a few feet away, but the damage was done. His helper ran for Hannah, but she was picking herbs and berries and stripping bark for basketmaking in a nearby woods, and he didn't find her until dark neared. Together, they fashioned a sled for Hiram from pine limbs and vines, managed to attach it to Abraham, and dragged him to the settlement.

Things that day had been a little strained between Hannah and one of the Waccamaw women, mostly because of Hiram being white. When Abraham dragged him into the encampment, the Waccamaw woman refused to admit the couple to their lodge. An argument ensued. Had Hiram been conscious, he would have probably shot the woman. The conflict quickly ended, however, when an angry Hannah switched the mule into dragging her husband to the tavern. There he slept on the floor for three days, unconscious from pain most of the time, and barely eating or drinking. On the fourth day, the Waccamaw woman appeared at the tavern door. She had been chastised by her husband for putting Hiram and Hannah out, and she was there to take them back. When they arrived at the lodge, the woman again refused to let them enter, insisting they sleep outside. The wife living in a lodge just south of that one heard Hannah arguing with the woman and admitted the couple into hers.

Until the accident, Hannah had been trading with both natives and whites in the village. Sassafras and willow were plentiful in the outlying area. She dried the sassafras root for tea and used stripped willow bark and the long willow stems to plait baskets, which she sold to a young trader. In turn, he bartered some to white settlers in Virginia, but most he sold to shippers taking native products to England. The work and injury had been as hard on Hiram as the trip to the coast; it took months for the leg to knit. By then, Hannah was growing homesick. Too, the add-ons at the tavern were now being completed by a group of Frenchmen bent on making their fortunes as trappers.

Hannah, during Hiram's convalescence, accumulated a modicum of wealth of her own. She traded her baskets for axe heads, grain, cloth, and cooking utensils from the French and English shippers, then these for more pottery from the Waccamaws. As Hiram regained his strength and mobility, he began using what remained of his money to buy lead, powder, and a few outdated rifles. With spring and the snowmelt disappearing from the distant mountaintops, he and Hannah packed Abraham and headed back to their home.

At the confluence of the Cape Fear and Black Rivers, they turned west through the meadowlands. For days, they trudged across country, and as the terrain began to lift, they entered the forests. Five days of picking their way through the trees and brush found them at an intersection of trails the natives used to follow game. They camped for the night. When they rose, Hannah began making coffee. She looked up to see Hiram taking his rifle from Abraham's still-loaded back.

"What is it, husband?"

He nodded to the west where a tall man stood in the trail, his own rifle cradled in the crook of an arm. The man wore baggy canvas pants and a deerskin shirt, his face pocked by a long-ago disease, probably smallpox. Then Hiram nodded in the opposite direction. Two more men, dressed similarly and equally pocked, stood there. The one to the west said something in a tongue Hiram couldn't translate.

"Do you understand him?" he asked of Hannah.

"A little. He's saying something about me."

Hiram turned and shot one of the two at their rear. The one to the west hurried a shot and hit Abraham in the flank, enraging the animal. He lumbered forward and reared at the man, who dropped his rifle and disappeared into the woods. The one remaining to the east had bent to his companion, and was having trouble rising. Something apparently wrong with one leg. Hiram found the already-loaded pistol on Abraham's back, aimed, fired, hit the man in his right shoulder. He limped off into the trees.

"Hannah, bare your knife! If one of them comes for you, defend yourself." Hiram quickly loaded both weapons, jammed the pistol in his belt. "We will eat later, as Providence dictates." She poured out the heated water, packed their bedrolls and cooking utensils while Hiram stalked into the woods a short distance, looking for the remaining men. They had stolen away, and as the couple resumed their trek, Hiram explained to Hannah that they were surely looking to kidnap her, sell her to renegade whites as a slave.

"The Waccamaw would not do that," she said, "and neither would the Catawba. Unless they were at war and took captives to add to their people, but even then, they would be adopted. Why do you say this?"

"They have learned white men's ways," Hiram muttered.

The wound in Abraham's flank was superficial, but it slowed the beast, and their travel became more deliberate. For the remainder of the day, they encountered no one else. That night, Hiram lay on the ground, feigning sleep. It was only in the hours before dawn that he fell into a wary slumber.

As they entered the hills rising toward the mountains, they stopped often for a day to rest and hunt. On one such stop, Hannah unpacked the cargo Abraham carried, and found that during the encounter with the three would-be attackers, some of the pottery she had bartered for was broken. She began to cry.

Hiram had returned with a pheasant, and he stopped plucking feathers. "What troubles you, wife?"

"The pottery," she sobbed, "it was so beautiful, and now most of it is either broken, chipped, or cracked. I did so much work to buy them."

Hiram did a most uncharacteristic thing. He rose and hugged her to him. "I am sorry for your loss."

"Our loss," Hannah replied.

"It will prove to be our loss, yes, but I could have lost you in the bargain. It is through the grace of Providence that I did not."

Six weeks later, they arrived at the five ridges settlement only to find abandonment and destruction.

Sixteen

"She's losing weight, Mr. Hardaway," the head nurse told me.

I dropped the phone from my ear, and sat at the breakfast bar, eyes closed. I wanted to acknowledge the nurse's statement, but my throat tightened. I couldn't speak. Too, I really didn't know what to say. As days passed, every occasional report was pretty much the same: either off or on the ventilator, she was being fed by a feeding tube, but despite that, or because of it, she was losing weight. Not dramatically, a pound every three or four days. Some in the ward recovered from the virus and were sent to a quarantine facility for two weeks. A few died. And then there was Angie. She never really improved, and she never worsened. Just the incremental weight loss.

I finally managed, "Is she going to die?"

"That's completely out of our hands," the nurse replied. "Normally, a COVID patient of ours will get well and be sent home. A few we don't save, as you probably know. But then —"

"But then Angie's isn't a normal case, right?"

"Yes."

"All right, thanks. Any significant news, one way or the other, please have someone let me know."

She replied noncommittally, and I hung up, thought about working, decided I couldn't. But I needed to; some of my clients were placing sympathetic calls, but they always asked when I'd get around to their taxes or other accounting issues they had engaged me to take care of. No, I had to work. I brought my laptop to the kitchen, sat again at the breakfast bar. The project I most needed to move forward was one a lawyer had given me, an accounting of the estate for the lawyer's oldest client. I opened the digital files her bank and stock broker had sent. It wasn't my task to delve for more wealth; instead, I was to certify that the wealth listed in the client's will was real, and in the amounts specified. Then the lawyer could distribute according to the deceased woman's desires.

As I went back and forth between the bank and stock data and the will, I stopped at one item the will described. A piece of property near Asheville, noted only by the land lot number, was to be held in trust until the deceased client's niece was twenty-one, at which time she had the option of taking possession of the land or selling it. It wasn't my responsibility to check the deed to make sure the land was still in proper hands, but I did. Initially ignoring the land parcel's description, I sought and found the listed owner's name. It wasn't the client. Nor was it the person managing the trust, in this case, the client's lawyer. A quick call to the lawyer revealed that I had an old copy of the will, which documented this property erroneously as belonging to his client. He had no idea how his client had claimed it in the first place. He was the second lawyer representing this client, he said, and the error must have occurred during his predecessor's representation. Buncombe County had now attached the property.

Who is this owner of record, I thought, this Jetty Wellington Almander? So I began a search for her, and eventually found old records of the property in Jetty's brother's name, one Hargrove Wellington. Wellington had died some two hundred and fifty years earlier, and the property was never sequestered by the State of North Carolina, which was odd. I began searching for the Wellingtons' heirs. Nothing. That made sense; if there had been, someone would have taken over ownership in a reasonable amount of time following one or the other's death. Still, there must have been a reason why the land hadn't been claimed by North Carolina so long ago.

Later, I found mention on a history website of a Wellington owning property in Buncombe County. On a genealogical website, I managed to trace that Wellington family to Hargrove. That led me to a family history website. As related there, the story began when Hargrove's sister married a neighbor living on adjacent acreage. She claimed that Hargrove had promised, and did give, the property to her as a wedding present, something Hargrove vehemently denied:

Our progenitors could not resolve ownership among themselves, so Jetty Wellington Almander, sister of Hargrove, sought resolution from a circuit judge, Jeremiah Horne.

"Is there a will?" asked Judge Horne. "Or some other document attesting to at least a promise of ownership?"

"None exists," admitted Jetty.

"Then you will have to resolve this among yourselves," Horne declared. "Upon my return east, however, I will enter into records held by the State of North Carolina this land as being in the name of Hargrove Wellington. That shall be your starting point."

"But what does that mean?" asked Jetty.

"You will have to procure the services of a lawyer," said Judge Horne. "With the ownership formally established as your brother's, you are encouraged to resolve the issue of the wedding gift with him. If you receive satisfaction in that regard, then the lawyer may draft an ownership document in your name."

"Your Honor, he has already assured my husband and me that he will not do that."

According to Jetty Almander's documentation of this exchange, in her own careful handwriting, Judge Horne did in fact register ownership of the land in the name of her brother, Hargrove, who continued to deny her ownership of the land, due to her husband James being a gentleman of color. Later letters written by Jetty and James Almander's son documented that his parents submitted a lien against the property. A circuit judge eventually granted the Almanders ownership, but then they moved to a settlement near what is now Hendersonville. They worked there, bought land, and farmed for the better part of their lives together. While writing this family history, we turned up a letter Jetty wrote to the son concerning this family incident. In it, she claimed the reason they moved to the farmland they lived on for most of their lives was that they determined the once-disputed land was located on a series of hills and ridges with swales among them, making the land inhospitable to either a growing family's residence or to mass cultivation.

Odd, I thought, to have filed a lien, have it legally

supported, doubly so since the land seemed worthless to them. But something in the story nettled. I looked back to the deed description as it was filed by Judge Horne and carried forth in Buncombe County land records. It was some ten miles overland from the confluence of the (French) Broad and Swannanoa Rivers, near a tributary of Rims Creek, later Reems Creek. This distance to the land lot was later disputed by state surveyors, who placed it more precisely a mile and a half from the intersection of U.S. Highway 23 and Wagner Branch, a southerly tributary of Reems Creek.

On reading this, my eyes widened. I opened an Internet map of the area, and there it was. The land was at least a portion of Catawba Corners Subdivision.

Now I felt compelled to find out more. Were any descendants of the Wellingtons on record, or for that matter, were any alive? An extensive search deep into the night unearthed no one. Maybe, I thought, I should search for the Almander family's descendants.

At that point, though, it was nearing midnight and I could hardly keep my eyes open. I fell asleep on the couch.

Morning flooded the ridges, and birds began their serenade. Flowers spread their naked beauty before the sun, but I couldn't bask in all of this. Angie was sick, and there was this genealogical odyssey I was on.

Then a surprise; I called the hospital and received what seemed encouraging news. Angie's condition was stable this day, but nothing significant had really changed, for better or worse. I could neither comfort her nor help with what I still hoped would be her recovery, so a quick cup of coffee and a piece of cheese toast, and my laptop took me to a genealogical website. An hour of searching through male descendants of James turned up nothing promising. I began the more difficult search of sisters and wives. Most of the day passed, revealing nothing. I ordered pizza. When it came, I opened a beer, the oven-warm treat at my other elbow, and continued my search.

Somewhere in the morass of marriages, divorces, deaths, and names, I stopped, smiled, put the pizza slice I'd just bit into back in the box. Now I had it. I knew Willard's preoccupation with the archaeological findings in the neighborhood were only part of his interest here. It was a connection distant by successive marriages, but Willard was a descendant via marriage of James Almander, and that could potentially put him in the line of ownership for property within Catawba Corners Subdivision. This, I suspected, was the real reason for Willard's paper. The county person allowing Marcus Blakely to buy the property had taken the easy way out, thinking there was no claimant to the property. This person had a judge assign ownership to Buncombe County, which sold the property to Blakely for a song.

Could Willard really claim to be legal heir of the Catawba Corners property? That would entail a massive search through family histories and wills, but I had a more fruitful idea. I would call Willard. Surely, since his now-and-again presence here was hardly coincidental, he would know whether he had legal claim to any of these properties. If he did, was he going to complicate life further for the residents? As I reached for my cell, it rang.

Seventeen

$\mathcal{A}$ new voice from Mission Hospital, a male nurse: "The ICU head nurse asked me to call you, Mr. Hardaway. Angie is to be moved to a step-down ward this afternoon."

For a moment I couldn't breathe. Angie was going to live! "When?" I gasped. "When can I see her?"

"Not for a couple of days, I'm afraid."

"But you just said —"

"She's still very weak. The doctors are confident she'll come around soon, but she's had a rough time with this virus. What she needs now is rest and quiet, and then there's still the virus to worry about. You wouldn't mean to, of course, but if she were to be re-infected, we might lose her. I'm sorry, but no visitors until the doctor says she's strong enough and her immune system is in better shape."

I thanked him and hung up. For the first time in days, my pursuit of Willard's history and this newfound connection to Catawba Corners didn't matter. But I did try to work. I did, I really did. I needed to show my clients some tangible progress, but I still couldn't manage it. So I grabbed an apple and took a walk.

A rainstorm had swept through Asheville in the night,

and the sky had cleared to a Pacific blue, the deep, rich sort that makes you think you can reach into it and touch the moon. The sun had risen high enough to flaunt its silver sheen and chase the remaining cloudy wisps away. A soft breeze, tinged with the faint aroma of honeysuckle, moved the early morning's coolness past me. A bluebird trilled nearby, but I couldn't locate her. I hadn't thought to put on my boots, and the grassy dampness gave my athletic shoes a chilly feel.

Then hoarse breathing and the sounds of rapid movements behind me. I admit I was trespassing as I walked up hill and down swale, but I hadn't expected to be overtaken by a horse. The Arabian mare trotted past, turned, stopped and stood, evaluating me.

Oh. The scent of my apple had drawn her. I took another bite, leaving half the apple intact. I held it on an extended palm and whistled. She approached, took the apple, her jaw sawing back and forth for the few seconds it took for the fruit to disappear. Another, softer whistle brought her a step closer, and I ran a hand down her back's slight concavity, then her neck. I probably imagined it, but I could have sworn she smiled. Then she dipped her head and pranced away.

As I continued my walk, Angie's image appeared before me, the ethereal presence gaunt, frail, but smiling. Will she look so emaciated when I finally see her? I knew about the weight loss, of course, but I hadn't really considered the damage the virus would have inflicted on her body's immune system. I had to be prepared for a worn and ragged Angie when they did finally allow me to see her. She would need me happy to see her, upbeat, not traumatized by a first view of her virus-ravaged body. Could I do that? Of course I could, so as I retraced my route home, I pictured her in a hospital bed, a wasted fraction of her original self. Then an idea.

I'd go now, cajole them into letting me see her. Maybe that would provide us both with an emotional boost.

I had thought to pocket my car keys and wallet before the walk, so I opened the garage, clambered into the Jeep and drove toward town and the hospital. The half-apple hadn't come close to tamping down my appetite, so I made an impromptu stop at a local beanery and ordered a very early takeout lunch; brunch the person at the window kept calling it — a pastry and fruit dish, along with two soft-boiled eggs in a plastic, goblet-shaped dessert glass. Oh, and a steaming mug of very aromatic decaf. It always surprised me that these humble edifices housing many of Asheville's eateries could summon the most delectable meals. I parked, wolfed that down, ordered another pastry and coffee, luxuriating in the taste, the aromas, and set sail for the hospital.

The remaining drive to Mission Hospital only took ten minutes. Given the time of day, I expected to park in the upper region of the deck across from the main entrance, but the surface level only contained a half-dozen autos. An improvised kiosk had been set up at the main entrance, the nurse there draped in PPE, her personal protective equipment, with one of those face protective devices that resembles an astronaut's helmet. I approached, pulling on my paper mask.

"Name, please," she said as she jabbed a thermometer at my forehead, read it, jabbed again, nodded, and scribbled on a loose-leaf sheet in an open binder.

I told her.

She had been looking at the notebook page, but as I gave my name, she eyed me for a moment, turned away, and made a phone call. Wheeling back, she said in a PPE-muffled voice I could barely understand, "Someone will be with you in a moment." Two minutes passed, then her phone rang. A grunt and a nod, and she hung up, her eyes never leaving me. "It'll be a few minutes, Mr. Hardaway. If you'd like to wait here, you can. Or you can walk, oh, say, down to the end of the parking deck and back, and someone should be with you then."

I shuffled off the hundred or so yards to the end of the parking facility and returned. A woman in business attire waited. A bald man dressed more casually stood at her side. Both wore face coverings. The woman introduced herself as Sheila Acuff. I turned to the man and, not thinking, extended a hand. He nodded, backed a step away, and looked to the woman.

She introduced the man as Jason Brownell, then said, "Let's sit in the lobby for a moment, shall we?"

As she opened the lobby door, I noticed the name tag on the Brownell fellow indicated he was the hospital chaplain. I knew without things playing out what this was about, but sometimes you have to let people do their job. I stepped inside and waited. These two hadn't been at this task long enough to forestall its innate awkwardness, and they both shuffled nervously, each waiting at the obligatory six-foot distance, I suppose, for the other to say what must be said in such circumstances. The damned virus! It would have been easier if Ms. Acuff had been allowed to grasp my hand, Brownell to grip my shoulder in brotherly fashion. But that wasn't to be. Finally, Brownell nodded to Ms. Acuff.

"I really don't know how to tell you this, Mr. Hardaway," she began, her eyes reddening. "We thought we had your wife —"

"Angie," I interrupted, already mildly angry with grief, "her name is Angie."

"Yes, of course, I'm sorry. We thought we had Angie through the crisis."

"The doctors are very capable," said the chaplain.

"Yes," the Acuff woman went on, "the staff thought she was through the crisis, and she was…"

At that point she couldn't hold back tears, and neither could I. Brownell took over, saying, "She was, Mr. Hardaway, but she had been weak for so long, you know? It was her heart, I'm afraid. She had a heart attack, and the doctors couldn't resuscitate her."

I turned my back to him. I'm not sure why. Maybe so he wouldn't notice the extent of my grief. I mumbled some now-forgotten thing and turned to them once more.

Ms. Acuff gathered herself and asked, "Do you wish to talk to one of the attending doctors?"

"No. I'm sorry, ma'am, but I want to go home now."

"Of course. Would you like for Mr. Brownell to escort you to your car, or maybe get your car for you?"

I said no and gave them a smile before leaving, but I'm sure it seemed fake. Actually, I don't remember driving home. I don't remember anything at all of that moment except for the numbness of loss.

Eighteen

Days passed into nights. I was only aware of nightfall, dawn, occasional hunger and thirst. My work remained in a languished state. I kept to myself, which wasn't too hard. My cloistering certainly didn't draw the curiosity and concern of neighbors; COVID was running rampant. At first, when the virus hit, people stayed home. Feeling cooped and cramped by the quarantining, many hit the streets again. Building materials warehouses and supply stores soon grew packed with people tired of playing Monopoly, backyard football and basketball, and watching TV movies with the kids. They edged out to buy craft supplies, building materials, tools, how-to books. Now they were home again, this time painting closets, repairing sagging doors, replacing toilet fixtures, taking up woodwork — anything to stave off boredom.

After a month, and well into the swelter that sometimes comes to late spring, I decided to take up wood carving. One afternoon at Lowe's, I was peering through fogged glasses at a tiny sign below a finished pine bin, when a familiar voice asked, "You need help building something?"

I turned to see Willard. I should say, I saw something like half of Willard. I had always seen him in my home environs, but now, on neutral turf, he looked emaciated. Hip bones probed upward from his jeans, shoulders drooping, shirt hanging on his frame like an oversized sheet. He started to say something, didn't. He cleared his throat behind a barely hanging paper mask.

"I heard about your wife," he said. "A terrible thing."

By now I'd experienced the struggles clients and a few friends put themselves through in trying to say something sympathetic. Strangely, Willard's heartfelt comment struck me as weirdly humorous, and I conjured a throat clearing to cloak an upwelling burble of laughter. "Thanks," I finally said. That summoned the throat lump that had, since Angie's passing, preceded tears. I blinked away wetness and managed to add, somewhat testily, "And, yeah, the doctors still don't know how to deal with it."

He nodded. "Look, if you need anything, or if there's anything I can do for you — you know, just call."

I smiled, but there was no way he could have seen it. My mask, one of a hundred a client had sent as a gift, was getting wrinkled, not to mention a trifle smelly. Sad that the pandemic closed off the fail-safe facial expressions that usually work when words fail us. I was pining for Angie, would be for many tortured months. It was in moments like this that I began to hate the ritual initiated by those trying to offer a few words of succor.

He started on his way, then turned back. "Oh, hey, Mr. Hardaway, I know your mind's on other things, but have you had a chance to read through those history paper chapters?"

It was an honest request, one I would have been able to respond positively to in any other circumstance. "No," I said, "I'm sorry, but Angie's sickness and all…"

"Right. I was just wondering." He started away again, stopped again. "I was wondering because I'm thinking about buying into your neighborhood, and —"

I waved both hands frantically, an odd happenstance for someone as undemonstrative as I tend to be. "I need to talk to you about that, but not now, okay?" I knew that would seem rude, so I added, "I need to get my ducks in a row. That is, some of the facts about what you've written."

His eyes widened a bit and I thought I saw the impression of a knowing smile beneath his mask. "Right. Be glad to talk anytime."

We would talk soon, certainly before the neighbors found out what I knew about his connection to Catawba Corners, and I needed to get to work on my part of the documents that, for me, drew Willard closer to the neighborhood. Angie would be haunting my thoughts for a long while, but I was now resolved to work.

If I hadn't been in such a morose mood when I saw Willard that day, I would have followed up on my intention to ask him whether he was aware of his potential ownership in Catawba Corners and whether he planned any legal action because of it. But I couldn't pursue it in that moment. Besides my newfound resolve to work, I was still preoccupied with the aftermath of Angie's burial: obtaining death certificates, closing her bank accounts, notifying old friends and relatives. I just couldn't be concerned with Willard.

I had planned not to have a service for Angie, and that caused quite a moment between Evie, Ben, and me. Evie's always been a bit mousy, Ben the plotter-disrupter. They kept insisting on a service of remembrance, almost five weeks after the fact, and I gave in.

They arrived the night before the service from Fayetteville, Arkansas, where Ben has his legal practice. I had arranged for them to stay at a local motel, but Ben insisted on staying at our house. I ushered them into the living room, directed them to the couch so I could stand the appropriate six feet away. Ben headed straight for my recliner, and I retreated toward the kitchen.

"What are you moving away from me for, Warren?" he said, with one of his I'm-better-than-you looks. "I don't have the virus. And take off that goddamn mask. You're in your own home for chrissake."

I was feeling down, and when I'm down, it doesn't take much to set me off. Ben's argumentative comment was just the ticket to put me in a state of combat. "You know for sure you don't have COVID?" I asked, my voice replete with sarcasm. "You were tested the day you left, I assume."

His sneer grew. "You know as well as I do that the tests are bogus. But to reply more directly, no, we haven't been tested. You can just take my goddamn word for it that neither of us has been in a position to get that fucking virus."

"Honey," Evie said, "please…"

His head snapped around to her and those snake eyes sent tangible darts her way. No wonder she's so mousy. "You watch, Evie, he's going to make a big fucking deal out of this virus thing. Hell, he believes this virus is bullshit as much as we do, but he doesn't want us in Angie's house, so he's wearing that stupid mask and is going to try to send us to some fucking roach motel where we can sleep in a pile of bedbugs."

What was it Shakespeare said about lawyers? I know, the popularity of it was a misinterpretation, but it certainly applies in Ben's case. "You're right, I don't want you in my house," I all but shouted at Ben. "If Evie had come by herself, I'd be happy to have her here. But you're such an unbearable shit." Here I was, sadly, cursing my way down to Ben's level, but I couldn't seem to help it.

Evie stamped the carpet so hard the room reverberated. But which side was she going to take in this set-to? "My dear friend just died, Ben, and I'll never see her again," she said in a loud, hurt voice. Then she turned to me. "We're here because I wanted, I needed, to honor her, so will you please just tell us what you have planned, so we can do that?"

Wow. I had no idea Evie had that in her. Even Ben seemed taken aback. So I told them I'd arranged for them to stay at a motel not far away, had checked around to pick the one that was doing the most to sanitize their facilities, had their employees tested, took customers' temperatures, and asked the obligatory questions before they could stay there. "And, Ben," I concluded, "don't even think about making such a fuss there that they won't let you stay, because you're sure as hell not going to have my house as Plan B."

With that, Ben sprang from the recliner, snatched Evie from the couch and strode to the door without a word. Good, I thought, I won't have to see Ben again, except maybe at the cemetery.

Wrong.

I cajoled the funeral home chaplain into joining us, asked him to say a few nice words about Angie at the gravesite. He added a brief comment about the toll COVID was taking on Asheville, which set Ben on edge, and then Ben grabbed my sleeve, said he had something to discuss, and they followed me back to the house. We went through the same placement game as the night before, Ben in my recliner, Evie on the couch. Then he dropped a bomb on me.

"Before Angie became really sick," he said in a quiet but firm voice, "she called Evie, said she was going to leave her part of the house to us. So I told Evie —"

"Hold on, Ben, I said, "there's no way she would do that. First, we have a will that clearly leaves all her possessions to me, except her clothes, which will go to Evie, if she wants them."

"You hold on, hotshot," said Ben. "I anticipated this reaction when Angie brought it up with Evie, so I asked her for a copy on the will. I made sure to date Angie's amended request after the will's date, with the obvious proviso that her request supersedes appropriate portions of the will." He leaned back with an all-conquering look.

Son of a bitch. I looked to Evie who, noticing, actually winced and turned away. You don't have to be an expert in body language to know Ben was lying. Evie knew it and was having a hard time abiding it. "And I suppose you have a copy of that document on you," I said.

He reached to his coat pocket. "I have the original, and you may see it. But you're sure as hell not going to have it. Or copy it, so you can falsify it." He drew out the paper, unfolded it, stood, and held it so I could read it.

I read the paper to the bottom. "That's not Angie's signature," I said. "That's not the way she signed her name." It was perhaps a second in duration, but Ben's eyes flashed and he looked to Evie, who, surprise, seemed to be enjoying the moment. She had sabotaged Ben's scheme with a clearly faked signature.

The doorbell sounded, my shoot-out with Ben in abeyance for the moment. Willard, frowning self-consciously, held up a paper, and I stood aside for him to enter the foyer. "I should have mentioned this when I saw you last, Mr. Hardaway," he said. "You've no doubt read that not only does my family lineage go back to this locale, but one of my forebears once owned the property here."

I looked over my shoulder, noticed Ben, ear cocked, trying his best to listen in. "Yeah," I said, "I have, but we had a service for my wife today. Can we talk about this some other time?"

"Absolutely," said Willard. "I just wanted to come by and give you a heads up."

"About what, exactly?" I was beginning to get a little annoyed with Willard, particularly with Ben listening.

"Just wanted to give you this paper," said Willard. "No big deal. Nothing has gone forward yet."

"Just tell me, okay?"

"All right, well, it turns out I definitely am the sole remaining heir to my forebear's title to part of Catawba Corners, and your house is sitting smack dab in the middle of it."

A chortle from Ben.

"You have to be kidding," I said to Willard.

"No, I'm afraid not. As I said, nothing legal has gone forward yet, just wanted to let you know." He shuffled his feet and edged toward the door. "You know, as a courtesy."

A courtesy? To tell me that he intends to take ownership of the land my home sits on? On the day we honored Angie? "You're very kind," I said acidly, but from his blank look, I could tell that went right by him. He turned, bumped his head on the door's edge, stumbled out and away.

"Well," said Ben, "sounds as though there's some competition for ownership of your house."

"You're right, Ben, it is my house. But no, there's no competition at all. The paper you're holding is made up, with a signature forged so poorly I can easily prove it. I don't know why you wanted to do this, but if you take it one step further, I'll see you to court. I'll win, and you'll be disbarred."

Another smile flashed across Evie's face. Ben's Adam's apple bobbed for a moment.

I turned to Evie and said, "I wish you could stay a while, I truly do, but I imagine when I see Ben to the door, he'll want you with him. Ben?"

Ben sighed, rose, flicked a finger in Evie's direction, his command for her to follow. She rolled her eyes, probably as much rebellion as she could muster, and trotted along after him. At the door, she stopped, turned, and hugged me, planted a slobbery kiss on my cheek. Then they were gone.

Nineteen

I collapsed into my recliner, read Willard's document, then read it again. I wanted to do something, anything but obsess over the claims to Angie's and my home, but this was all I found myself doing. Deep into swirling thoughts, I must've gone into a trance state of some sort, because the next time I looked around, the sun was slipping beyond the mountains on the western horizon, leaving a magnificence of hues. Ben would probably make a Hail Mary try to screw me out of Angie's portion of the house, but I had no idea what Willard would end up doing. Finally, and that was the moment I really realized what a nocturnal person I am, I leaped to my feet, made a pot of coffee. Rejuvenated by the nutty beverage, I dragged out my copy of the home property deed and ancillary papers.

Aha, I remember now! The house and property were in my name only. It had been a sore point between Angie and me for a while. Actually, the marriage seemed to be in jeopardy then, one reason we moved from Raleigh to Asheville — a new start, and all that. So I was paying the mortgage in toto when we moved in, and the full down payment on the loan. We'd had a huge fight about not including her name on the title, but it had been inconvenient to do so when we applied for the home loan. We lived in an apartment here before the construction began, and I was just starting to amass clients, barely enough to have the income needed to qualify for the mortgage loan. Angie was painting then but not selling any, and listing her as a co-payer on the loan would have been a liability, probably costing us the loan. I guess she must've fretted quietly about that for some time. Later, she approached me about putting the house in both our names. I confess, I didn't want to; my first wife had insisted when we were divorcing that she get the house, even though she didn't earn much, didn't pay any of the bills, only living there for the few months of our marriage, and the judge granted her that. I still had to pay the mortgage for her until such time as she remarried. Fat chance, lesbians marrying back then! As a result, I lived in a landscaping warehouse after we split until I could find a cheap place to rent. There was no way I wanted to go through that again, so I consulted a lawyer about the path forward. She was nice, listened quietly, and then suggested I work something out informally with Angie, something that would blunt her concerns. And once, just once, we, Angie and I, openly talked our way through a serious issue.

"You know I want the best for you, for both of us, don't you?" I asked.

"And you know that if we divorce, or for some reason you die first, I won't be able to make it on my own as an artist, don't you?" she replied, wadding and un-wadding a tissue as we talked.

I nodded and plunged on. "You know I love you, that I'd never want to live without you."

She looked to her lap. "Yes."

"Do you trust me to do the right thing?"

That brought a sharp look, and it was a moment before she answered. "You've never given me reason not to."

"Here's what I'd like to do, then. I'll take out a cash life insurance policy on myself, with you as beneficiary, as much of one as I can afford. If we divorce, you can take out an amount that will allow you to buy a condo or a small house. If you can afford to repay that over time, great. If you don't choose to repay it completely, you'll still have some life insurance on me, and you're not out anything."

A nod, eyes glistening.

"As a hedge, we can go to the bank tomorrow and start a savings account in your name. Every month, starting next month, and unless things get tight and I can't afford to, I'll put a couple hundred dollars in it, so if something happens between us, you'll have that. I'll keep the house in my name, and it'll stay that way if we've divorced in the interim. If we're still married, our will says the house will be yours. That way, if I do die early and we're still married, that's one thing you won't have to deal with, except formally changing the name on the title."

"You'll still support me and my art, the way you've done since we married?"

"I'm afraid so," I said, smiling.

I'm not sure she got my smart-assed reply as willing agreement; she daubed an eye with the tissue.

"Unless you have a better suggestion," I added.

"No, that's fine. It-it's wonderful, in fact." She reached for me and we hugged, Angie crying. "I've never had a man offer something like that," she whispered. "You'll really do it, won't you?"

"Yes, of course. I will do it. I want to do it."

And I did. I bought the policy, a huge one, and every

month, during the time prior to her sickness, I put as much money as I could afford into her account. It turned out to be our only savings, but I was glad to provide for her security and mine in a way that didn't threaten our mutual well-being. Oh, I had to start budgeting more deeply, but that was fine. Too, it made me hustle to find more work. The lawyer was right; sometimes, if a couple love one another, you just have to work things out based on some semblance of trust. After that, she was happier, the lovemaking was better for both of us and, with that resolution accomplished, her artwork flourished. With my added work load and for the first time since we bought the house, we actually had some mad money.

So that was one bird down. Ben would have a hell of a time getting anything from me concerning the house, even if some judge did buy into his bogus paper. Now on a roll and duly excited, I would talk with Willard, find out what he was planning to do.

I realized as I began to hunt for him that I had no idea where he lived or worked, and it was a while before I was able to track him down. Actually, he found me. I had put the finishing touches on my analysis of the main client's will I'd been working on for so long during Angie's sickness, and was admiring the hefty payment the surviving family had just placed in my bank account when the doorbell rang.

Willard and I sat in the kitchen, and I poured coffee for both. He had recently been tested, had proven uninfected, and I hadn't been out of the house for over a week, except to take a few solitary hikes, so we went without the masks.

"I heard you were looking for me, Mr. Hardaway," he said, "so I decided I'd better let other things lie and get in touch. You're concerned about a lawsuit involving your property, I guess."

I was, of course, but in that moment, my exhilaration cooled, I didn't want a heated discussion over home ownership. So I smiled and said, "Just curious, Willard, about the history of the place. But, yes, I should know what legal steps you're considering."

He returned the smile, and seemed, for the first time ever, to be at ease. "Please call me Jeff. My full name is Jeff Willard. Jefferson Almander Willard."

Well I'll be darned. I was just now accepting that he was the genuine article. He'd never given me reason to think otherwise, I suppose, but when someone waltzes into your life, no matter how little involvement that entails, the human tendency is to be a little wary at first. Now he had me at ease. "Then stop this Mr. Hardaway thing and call me Warren."

We chatted inanely for a while. Then we edged into the history of the place, but more on that in a bit. I topped off his coffee. After he sipped, he said, "I'll have to admit I was on shaky ground when I said my ancestors' claim to the property here involved only your home. Actually, it had initially. My family built a sawmill here, which set up shop right on your house's site, when the creek tributary had a lot more water running through the property. The sawmill was new technology at the time and it burned at some point. A brother of the relative who built the sawmill, Andrew, came here to run it, and he and his wife lived in an attached house. They died in the fire. No one else ever claimed the property. I feel that the county had no right to attach that part of the subdivision and sell it to your developer."

"You feel you have a legal claim to the property here, then?"

He sipped his coffee once, twice, then a third time

before answering. Coffee can loosen tongues more quickly than booze once a person is at ease in a conversation, but that didn't seem to work on Jeff Willard. He was, and is still, I imagine, a thoughtful, cautious man.

"I hated to, but I hired a lawyer," he said. "This sort of thing can be so convoluted, and to be honest, for me it's a distraction. I just want to pursue the archaeology and history."

I nodded, waited for more, but no more was forthcoming without prodding. "Where do you think your property limits are, then?"

He shrugged sheepishly to punctuate his growing indifference to all but the history of the place. "Most of my claim lies next to the road," he said. "Down where the neighborhood seem to want to build. The common property there."

I had to stifle a laugh, but a chortle squibbed out despite my effort. "The neighborhood's been at one another for months over that property. Some want to build a clubhouse and pool there, but others don't want it at all. In fact, the naysayers are just about willing to go to war with the rest over it."

"It's that bad?"

"Yep. And here you come, muddying the waters for both sides."

He buried his face in the thin fingers and bony palm of one hand. "You see, this is exactly the sort of thing I didn't want to deal with. I really can't afford the expenses of litigation. The deed search and possibly a brief court appearance is all my wife and I can afford."

"My opinion?" I offered. "I think, given what the county did in taking possession, that may be all it'll take." He gave me a puzzled look, so I told him of coming across his name as the only living person with anything resembling a claim to Catawba Corners.

"You've been reading my history paper, then." He asked for another cup of coffee, and as he stirred creamer into it, he said, "It's not so much that I want the property, you know? I just want to have it over with and get back to my work, although knowing I have this claim does keep me working here, on the archaeology." The need to work. Something I fully understood. "But," he added, "how do I get the other parties involved to let it go?"

"I'm not sure you can. This is a contentious time we live in, and these are contentious people. Both sides want what they want, and no one is willing to compromise."

"Ironic, isn't it?" he mumbled, shaking his head.

"So what's your end game? You just going to punt? Sounds like your heart isn't in this property thing."

He finished his coffee, waved off another refill, stood, and set his cup quietly in the kitchen sink. "I think I have to follow through. It's of a piece with my history of the ridges."

He asked again how much I'd read of his archaeological paper. I told him Hiram and Hannah had a difficult time of it in the low country, had headed back to the ridges, only to find the settlement destroyed. That's where we left our conversation, and after he departed and I'd done enough work to salve my conscience, I read more.

Twenty

"*H*iram?" Hannah asked. "What has happened?"

No response, only a crestfallen look as he took in what had been the settlement.

"Hiram?"

He absently put an arm over her shoulder, drew her close. "Nothing good, I'm afraid."

The settlement was no more. Their cabin had been burned. The other shelters had either been burned or torn down. From the looks of it, attackers tied ropes to some and pulled them apart. Cooking pots were strewn about, pottery broken. Windblown clothing pieces had been impaled by bushes, briars, and low-lying limbs. The remaining crops in the terraces had been burned. A few decaying bodies lay about, and a stench rose on a breeze drifting down the hollow between the two main ridges. The bodies of settlement dogs lay here and there, blood-caked holes in their sides and heads from rifle shots. This wasn't the work of a rival tribe.

Then, from their rear, raspy breathing. Two haggard boys, one perhaps fourteen, the other no more than ten, ran toward them, handcrafted knives in their hands.

"Stop!" yelled Hiram in their native language. He shoved Hannah behind him, stepped toward the oldest, who was in the lead.

But the boys didn't stop.

Hiram had just enough time to pick his rifle from their mule's back and swing it. The older boy's legs flew from under him. Seeing his brother go down, the younger boy stopped, knelt, and began to cry.

Hiram took the knife from the younger, then the injured one. He knelt over the oldest, who moaned in pain. A look of recognition slipped across Hiram's face, then fell to sadness. "I know you," he said. "You're the son of Aaron, aren't you?"

The near-starved boy nodded, then threw up bile. "I son of Yellow Bird. Aaron not his name. We take true names back."

Hiram sighed. He had given as many of the tribe's men Christian names as would take them, protection against settlers or hunters that might encounter the settlement and eager to kill natives as heathens.

The younger boy couldn't stop crying. Hannah hitched the mule to a low pine branch and knelt over him, drew him to her. He readily fell into her arms, crying with abandon.

"What happened here?" Hiram said to the older boy.

"White men," said the boy. "They wore…" Hiram waited as the boy struggled with his language's equivalent to the needed word. "…uniforms."

"Soldiers," said Hiram.

The boy nodded. "They say we steal from farmers. White farmers."

Hiram pointed southward. "That would be down along the river, a day's walk."

"Yes."

"But you didn't steal?"

He didn't answer directly. "No one here. We were…" Again, he struggled with the word. "…helpless. They called us names. Bad names." The boy looked toward Hannah and his brother, but the movement twisted his broken leg, and for a moment he cried, too. "We…we were ground bird hunting, caught nothing. They did not see us. We come back, hide, see them do this."

Hiram called out to Hannah to fetch the boys something to eat. Give them water first, he told her. They will throw up whatever you give them to eat otherwise. He gave the older boy a shot of whiskey, then another, straightened the broken leg as the boy screamed. He cut a sapling into two pieces and lashed them to the boy's leg with bits of rope.

"We cannot stay here, Hiram," said Hannah, while she made a soup of herbs and bits of venison. "The soldiers will come, or the farmers. They will think we are part of the settlement and they will kill us."

"Let me think on it," said Hiram, "but I believe we will have to stay here for a while. We need to rest. And I need to hunt. We must have food."

The boys ate ravenously late that afternoon. Hiram gave them each a second helping, but refused them more, insisting instead that they sip water, as much as they were comfortable downing. With the sun's demise that day, Hannah lit a fire from twigs, branches, and a partially burned piece of log from the cabin.

With the night's noises a backdrop to the fire's limber flames, Hiram smiled. Quite a sight to see, he thought; youth heal so quickly. They hardly give their minds to something that aging adults pray for. The older one, whom he insisted on calling James, toyed with the improvised crutch Hiram had made from a bifurcated hickory limb. The younger,

Andrew, as Hiram called him, looked longingly at the tin plate holding Hannah's almost untouched meal. Hiram called on her to quit her bustling with bedding, the night tarp she was slanting over saplings angled toward the fire. Rest, wife, he told her. We are all taken care of for the night, so please care for yourself. And eat. Down your food before Andrew does. She smiled at that, sat, and ate. For a while, the only sounds were the night noise, snaps and pops from the fire, and Hanna's fork occasionally scraping the tin plate.

Hiram called to the boys, who lounged on the fire's opposite side, to recount again, and in detail this time, the soldiers' attack on the settlement. The boys spoke warily at first, and then their chatter turned into a cacophony of confusing information.

"Whoa, now," laughed Hiram, "one at a time. Don't interrupt one another, and tell me, had the soldiers been here before?"

"It was maybe ten days before the attack," said James, nodding. He glanced to Andrew, who added his nod. "The old medicine woman, Broken Wing, she saw something in the trees."

Andrew nodded excitedly. "Yes, a pair of our men slipped into the woods and circled the settlement, saw four men in uniforms watching the village. They edged closer until they were between the soldiers and their horses. One of them turned, saw our men. They looked frightened. One drew his weapon. Our men stepped aside, and the soldiers mounted their horses and rode off."

"Did they speak to your men?" asked Hiram.

"They called them bad names," said Andrew.

"An-i-mals," James said carefully. "A-and the name they call the black slaves."

Hannah looked up from her plate, wiped her chin with a forearm, frowned.

"Yes," said Hiram, "Hannah has been called that. And me a time or two as well for marrying her. Please go on with the story. Were your people concerned that the soldiers had come?"

"We always welcome people traveling," said James, "but not everyone is friendly. We defend ourselves." He winced as he waved a hand to encircle the surrounding woods. "We settled here, these trees, this land. This is our home."

Hiram nodded. "There is much land, many trees and game animals. The ground is rich enough, even in these hills. There is land and game for all."

The boys scowled. "But that is not the way with your people," said James. "You do not respect the rights and the lands of others. I have heard many stories. Once I saw your people —"

"All whites are not my people," Hiram interrupted. His voice had begun to rise. He harrumphed and quieted. "We come from many places, we speak many languages, we have different customs and habits."

"We do, too," said Andrew. His expression now seemed a twist of confusion.

"How?" said James. "How is it that your people are different from us?"

"Whites were once like your people, I think," said Hiram. "I don't know, maybe we grew used to fighting, taking from one another, instead of respecting and cooperating. Not all whites are like the soldiers and those farmers. None of us are used to this land, to the people who were already here, and maybe we are afraid of you. I don't know."

James huffed. "Afraid? You have these big, strong

horses, and the weapons that bark before they kill. You're not afraid of us, your people are mean."

What James said was true, thought Hiram. We are generous to our kind, violent and mean to others. Our first thought of others is usually one of suspicion, but we're often innocent and gullible when thinking of those we believe we know. We are industrious and lazy, brave and fearful. We are impatient. We can be loving, but you don't want to ever cross us. We think nothing of killing, but we're afraid to die.

"Some are, indeed," said Hiram. "But this isn't the sort of land whites would want. Most whites want much land, flat land, so they can grow many things."

"Then why did they come here?" asked Andrew.

"The whites who came here first took the best land, brought the black slaves to do the work. But whites kept coming here, and now they move toward the place where the sun sets."

"There are that many?" asked Andrew.

"And more."

"So what are we to do, Hiram?" asked James.

"We will be here a while," he replied, glancing at Hannah. "When we feel we must leave, we'll take you with us."

They stayed, against Hannah's constant objections, for six months, living in an improvised shelter Hiram and Andrew made from the village lodges' remnants. During that time, a circuit judge became lost, encountered them, and stayed three days. Hiram urged the judge to assign him ownership of the ridges, and the judge was willing. But surveyors wouldn't be able to survey that area for years, until the army declared it safe for white settlers. The judge would describe the land Hiram wished to bear his name and leave it in the court records in New Bern, then the state's capitol. The survey was eventually carried out, but the survey only accounted for part of what is now the Catawba Corners acreage.

Five months into their stay, Hiram took the mule to a settlement near what is now Hendersonville, only to discover that a pair of buyers had traveled there from New Orleans, hoping to find cotton growing, something desperately needed in the low country to the east and south. During their two-week stay, one of the buyers, who had been coughing and seemed sickly, came down with a fever and died. Hiram left town once he had traded deerskins for the flour and cornmeal. Days later, he, Hannah, and the two boys abandoned the ridges and traveled north into Tennessee.

Yellow fever. I set the paper aside, surfed the Web for the disease, rubbed my eyes, and opened a beer. The disease had a spotty spread until the mid-1850s when it claimed a large portion of the southern U.S. Apparently slave ships became homes for mosquitoes, or slaves carrying the virus brought it from Africa to ports in the fledgling Colonies, where travelers, traders, buyers, and migrating citizens spread the disease. So that must have been why the land's title remained tenuous, with no one living on it after Hiram and Hannah's departure. Willard had told him in the course of conversation that he was born in Tennessee, so it would likely prove to be his land, but a serious legal debate over ownership was in the offing.

What should I tell the neighborhood association about Willard's land claim? he wondered. Or more to the point, should I tell them at all?

Twenty-One

*T*he question resolved the next day when the association president, Sadie Wilhoit, called on me. A tall woman, hardly fat, just big and gigantic of personality. I offered her a cup of coffee, which she turned down in rather brusque manner. I led her into the kitchen, where she perched on a stool at the bar, motioned me to the kitchen's far side, and asked, "I know this Willard fellow has been visiting you, so please don't deny it."

I smiled as I reached for my mask, said I had no reason to say otherwise, which sort of ruined her game plan, I think.

"I assume you're aware he's claiming ownership of our development."

"Not all, I believe, just part."

She sat up straighter. "So you knew about it, and didn't bother to notify the Board."

I had never encountered Sadie in an official confrontation, but from what Angie told me about her, there was no point in tilting for the high ground. Still, I couldn't let her feel she could walk all over me and, by association, Willard. "I've hardly had time to, Sadie. I only found out about it yesterday." I had to wave her quiet then in order to get in my counterattack. "So how is it you found out? As soon as I did, it seems." But she was way ahead of me; she bent for her purse, pulled out a letter, waved it, handed it to me.

I read it — a polite letter from Willard's lawyer, explaining the situation, claiming the developer never pursued a quit-claim deed. Nothing in the letter stated that Willard actually desired to take possession of the property.

"How dare you," she exclaimed, "conspire with an outsider to destroy our neighborhood."

I didn't intend to pursue her on that tack, I really didn't. "Sadie if you think that's what I've been up to, you have a loose screw."

She leaned forward, and said in precisely chopped off words, "Let me assure you, sir, that were the law to allow it, I'd sue you personally for this. As it is, I'm going to recommend to the Board —"

Thinking back now, I realize how depressed I remained over Angie's death, that she and I never had a chance to talk at the end, to say our goodbyes. I could have been more diplomatic that day with Sadie, more emotionally disciplined, but some days it just doesn't happen, particularly when you're in the throes of grief. What I said to her in reply doesn't bear repeating, in its precise and colorful verbiage, but it amounts to telling her to get out of my house, to stay away from it and me, and if she ever threatened to sue me again, or Willard, it would be me who took her total and entire self to court. Not the Board. Her. Strangely, my reply didn't further enrage her. Instead, fear seemed to shine in her eyes for the briefest of moments. She rose from the stool, backed away, turned to the door, and clomped down the front steps.

The next morning, I found my house had been egged, and wet toilet paper hung like Spanish moss from the jack pine next to the driveway. In addition, the fencing around Willard's dig was torn down, and someone had spray-painted GO AWAY on the Viking stone. No kids lived in the neighborhood then, so those childish acts had to have been performed by adults. I thought about calling the police, finally settled on my lawyer.

"If what you say is true, and there's no significant damage to your property, there's no remedy the law can apply for you," she told me. "What I can do is give you the name and number of a mediator, if you want it. He can referee your case and help both sides come to some sort of agreement."

It was hot that day. Her office sat on the west side of a building off Charlotte Street. The air conditioning was chugging away, but it wasn't a fair fight. I began to sweat. She handed me a box of tissues to swab the perspiration. "I know this woman," I told her, "at least by neighborhood reputation. She's tough as nails, won't give in once she's decided on a course of action."

"This mediator," she said, flipping through an old-fashioned Rolodex, "I feel confident he can help." She scribbled on the back of one of her cards, handed it to me.

With nothing else to say or do, I thanked her, rose, and left.

At home again, and dreading to get into another dogfight with Sadie so late in the day, I decided to finish reading Willard's paper.

Hiram put the boys to work helping him cut trees, and in a surprisingly short time they had amassed enough logs to build a new home. Meanwhile, mostly in the days' hours before sunset, they built a brush lean-to as a residence until the new home was finished.

One day Hiram and the boys returned from a morning-long hunting trip to find Hannah sitting on a stump at the edge of the clearing where their new home was rising, head to her hands. Hiram lifted her scratched and bruised face to meet his. Her yellow gingham dress had tears at the shoulder seams, and browning splotches of blood formed a willowy triangle down her lap.

"There are some women from across the hollow," she said. "They came to visit, said they wouldn't stand for letting an Indian live nearby. They said I would cause trouble. So I fought them, Hiram. I fought them." She reached for him, cried into one of his pant legs. When she had quieted, he instructed James to take a wooden pail to a nearby stream and fill it. A roasted rabbit leg remained in his poke, and after he washed away her spent blood and she had drunk her fill, he handed her the leg. It took only a short while for her to wipe her mouth with a tattered sleeve, drop the now-meatless leg bone, and offer a weak smile.

The women Hannah spoke of were part of a German clan, the Dekkers, who lived a mile and a half away through a pine and poplar forest. The patriarch was a cobbler who was having trouble finding business in settlements along the Tennessee River. His sons were struggling to learn farming, and they seemed to want to blame their difficulties on everything and everyone else.

"I have an idea," said Hiram. "Andrew, fetch the shovel. Go dig up a bucket of our potatoes and carrots. Hannah, if you're rested, pull some herbs. James and I shall clean the squirrels for you to make a stew."

While the others were going about their tasks, he built a fire in the middle of the clearing, set up the posts and crossbar for the iron cooking pot, then helped James with the skinning. It took two hours, the sun still above the trees when Hannah announced the stew cooked.

"Do not eat your fill," Hiram said. "Most of this we shall take to the Dekkers. The boys frowned and Hannah scowled. The meal over, Hiram told the boys to load their guns, pack an extra portion of wad, rifle balls, and powder. "And don't forget your knives," he told them. Hiram handed James his gun, and they shambled off toward the Dekker settlement.

As they neared the Germans' clearing, Hiram instructed the boys to hang back a few yards and to come forward only when he signaled. "Halloo!" he called out as he set the pot between his legs. A man's head appeared from the entrance to their ramshackle shelter. He spoke something to the occupants, then three Dekker men approached.

"My family thought since you were neighbors," Hiram said, "you might like some stew, so I had my wife Hannah make up some real special."

Hiram handed one a spoon and pointed to the stew, which he had now set between them. The man dipped, cautiously tasted, said something to the others in their native tongue, handed the spoon to another, and when all three had tasted, they smiled in unison.

"There's plenty for your family," said Hiram. "It's all for you." The gray-bearded patriarch approached and stood with the other Dekker men. He tasted. Then he nodded, smiled, and called the women and children, who wasted no time filling their metal bowls.

When they had eaten their fill, Hiram called the old man and his sons aside. "I expect you know what your women did this afternoon," he said. "But in case you do not, they came to our place while my sons and I were away, and they attacked my wife and beat her. He flicked a finger toward the woods, and the two boys walked from the leafy shadows. James handed Hiram his rifle.

"We aim to be good neighbors," said Hiram, "but if your women so much as act unfriendly to my wife, we will come back here, and we will kill you all, every man, woman, and child." He looked to James. "See the hat hanging on that pine branch?"

James nodded.

All turned to the tree-bearing hat, which was some thirty yards away. James put his rifle to his shoulder, bent to sight, and fired. The hat quivered and fell to the ground. One of the Dekker children ran to it, held it up, with a finger through the bullet hole.

"That was just so you understand I meant what I said," declared Hiram. "Like I told you, we mean to be good neighbors, so it's up to you how we treat one another."

The old man glared at his sons and the now-cowed women, and he nodded to Hiram. Hiram hefted the pot and he and the boys disappeared into the trees.

All well and good, and a most interesting story, I thought, but what, really, has this story to do with Willard? I had found no compelling connection to his rather distant Almander family ties that could realistically override in his favor the county's decision to sell the land to Blakely. Yet Willard had gone to lengths to establish a familial closeness to Hiram Rose in his paper. It seemed obvious that while Hiram had once established his ownership of the ridges, that had been lost in subsequent decades, at least by the time the quarrel over ownership of that land took place between the Almanders and Wellingtons. Well, this would have to be Willard's problem. If the ties binding these families and Catawba Corners existed, he'd have to assume the burden of proof.

Twenty-Two

$\mathcal{T}$he next Board meeting, held at Sadie's home, drew almost three-quarters of the residents. The house filled and everyone's temperature taken, residents elbow to elbow, most sitting on the floor, many standing in back. A tide of conversation rose. At exactly eight p.m., Sadie stood and said, "All right, all right, everyone shut up." Apparently rethinking her tone, she offered a smile that could have easily been called a grimace. A titter of complaining laughter began creeping through the Wilhoit living room. She silenced it with an upraised hand.

"We're dispensing with the usual business tonight to address a serious matter I unearthed, and yes, it's about Warren Hardaway's…" She paused for effect. "…and his late wife Angie's, home."

"Only indirectly," I said from my chair at the rear of the room.

She glared, then looked to her oaken floors, force-fed another faux smile. "I suppose you're right. It's a friend of Hardaway's, a Mr. Willard —"

"He's not really a friend," I said. "He showed up at my home a few times, with —"

"Will you stop interrupting?" Sadie yelled. An awkward

silence fell over the Wilhoit living room. "All right, then," she said, "as I was saying, a friend of Warren Hardaway's."

I stood. "I wouldn't call Willard a friend. He's an archaeologist who came here because of the Viking stone and, as you know, he's been remediating a Native American settlement site here. For some reason, probably because of my interest in his dig, he's taken me into his confidence."

That seemed to nonplus her a tad. She rephrased and then added that Willard and I had been plotting a takeover of the neighborhood. I had never retaken my seat, so I worked my way forward. "You just wait a minute," I said.

"Shut up and sit down," someone called out.

"Please, Warren," said Sadie's husband Ned, his voice trembling, the way I still imagine it does in conversations within the Wilhoit household, "can't we get through this with decorum? Let Sadie finish, won't you? Then you can have your turn."

He had a point. "All right, but get your facts right," I said, glaring all the while at Sadie. She wasn't cowed now; she had mustered her usual moxie and returned the look. I took my seat.

She began again, telling essentially the correct story. I could have interjected a correction or two, but didn't. The neighbors, most wearing COVID masks, began silently choosing sides in the still-embryonic set-to. Some would nod eagerly while the others tightened their jaws, huffed, or groaned exasperatedly. Hence my epiphany:

Few were listening to or even concerned with the factual nature of what was being said. They were simply going about the emotional calisthenics of choosing sides. As Sadie's harangue began to wind down, I thought about that. On what basis were these neighbors choosing whom they believed? Women are the social glue in relationships outside the nuclear family; the husbands, boyfriends, or live-ins generally go along with the flow of the women's social contacts, so that wasn't it. Was it gossip, then? Were increasingly embellished rumors flying about Angie, Willard, me? Again, as far as I was concerned, no way of telling. But as I considered it, their choosing sides had to do more with their backgrounds. Some in this middle-class neighborhood probably looked back on their pasts, their growing up, the misfortunes that had befallen their families, thus were sympathetic to anyone, such as me, who was being dumped on by people or forces beyond their grasp. Others, no doubt, breathed a sigh of relief in observing someone else's misfortunes, and piled on.

Sadie looked to her chair, prepared to sit, her oration over, when the doorbell rang. Ned, at the room's far side, glanced her way, asking through facial expression if he should let it go. Sadie gave him an exasperated, who-cares look.

Who was it? No one could have been more surprised than I when Ned returned with Willard in tow. The room hushed. Ned tried to direct him to his own chair. Instead, Willard made way through the living room and stopped beside Sadie.

"I don't know many of you," he began, "none, really, except for Mr. Hardaway here, but I have been in contact with some of you about my archaeological project. I heard through the grapevine that you were meeting here tonight, and you should understand that little bit of information didn't come from Mr. Hardaway."

He glanced to Ned, who shrunk a little, and that spoke volumes. I hoped no one else in the room noticed. Willard went on. "As I began researching the property here and what was found in the dig, I discovered increasingly familiar information. To make short a rather long story, I came to realize that my family had claim to at least some of the land here at Catawba Corners. I'm related to one Hiram Rose, who came here, to this very property, when it was an established settlement by a group of Catawbas, a tribal group of Native Americans. He and his wife, Hannah, were never able to have children of their own, but they did take in two boys from the tribe, James and Andrew. The family moved to Tennessee later, due to whites massacring most of the tribe's members."

"Hah!" said someone. "Then you don't really have claim to anything here."

"Actually, by some odd coincidence, my family claimed it twice. Hiram had his name placed on a deed of sorts after the massacre and filed at the state capitol. The four of them lived together in Tennessee until the boys were grown, but James seemed to have a visceral connection to the old tribal home, and he moved back. There were quite a few Roses living in the general area, and he really wasn't a Rose anyway, so he took the name Almander. It was a bit of irony on his part. When he returned, he found a large oak he remembered from the time after the massacre with the name Al Manger carved into it. The name, barely readable at that point, was apparently carved by one of the soldiers who had destroyed his people and their village. So he stuck the two names together, changed one letter, and he became James Almander."

Ah, I thought, his claim made more sense now, and so did his paper about Hiram. But will he claim the land?

"James tried to farm," he went on, "but the terrain was too forbidding for that to happen by the European means

Hiram had taught him, so he started a sawmill, brought his brother Andrew here to run it. There was another family living nearby, name of Wellington, and James courted one of the women in that family. Her brother, Hargrove, promised part of the land to her as a wedding present, then reneged on it when he found James was of Catawba heritage. Jetty, the wife, later established legal claim to it, but bad blood remained between the Wellingtons and Almanders. The Wellingtons coveted the sawmill because of its revenue potential, but Andrew fought them over it. At one point, they exchanged gunfire. The conflict escalated quickly. One night, a Wellington set fire to the mill, killing Andrew, his wife, and their two small children."

He paused, looked from face to face. I can only guess what he saw in those sixty-some mask-cloaked sets of eyes. Anger? Guilt? Indignance? Understanding? Sympathy? Sadie had taken her seat and was staring at the floor at her feet, brow in rows so deep you'd think potatoes could grow there. Willard continued.

"That said, I just want to reassure you all that despite whatever of my legal claims a court may recognize to your neighborhood land now, I have no intention of upsetting your lives." A sense of palpable relief took the room. He went on, talking more about his archaeology project, wound down, and declined an invitation to stay for refreshments before leaving.

"All right, then," said Sadie, "I guess that winds us up."

"Not quite," I replied. I had been toying with an idea most of the past two days, and after Willard's story, which incensed me and, I'm sure, some of the other residents, I decided to go forward with it. "Someone vandalized Willard's excavated work, which I'll remind you benefits the neighborhood because of its historical value. Then you T.P.ed and egged my property. You've tried to damage my reputation, and Angie's too, indirectly. This isn't the way neighbors should act. I took pictures of everything you did to my home and to Willard's project. A few of you made threats against us and our life here, and I documented those. My lawyer now has all of that." I scanned the room. Good. Frightened pairs of eyes. A few averted looks. I continued. "As a result, she's drawn up papers she will take to court next week in order to file a lawsuit against the current Catawba Corners Board of Directors for malicious intent to harm."

That caused quite a hubbub, and shouting ensued — at both me and Sadie. Strong Sadie, as we'd come to know her, couldn't stop it, and I let it go on for a while before shouting above the din that I had something more to say. I knew something few, if any, in the room realized — I had little chance of succeeding in such a suit. A judge would chastise the Board and tell us all to make nice with one another.

"I'll be willing to have her drop the suit," I began, "but I want something from all of you first." Here I looked directly at Sadie. A hum of conversation still lay across the living room, but it didn't last long, quickly coming to a ragged end. "Sometimes this sort of neighborhood bullying ends, only to start up again later, perhaps against the same resident. So I'm demanding something I hope will force you to be better neighbors in the future." From my jacket pocket, I drew an addendum to my lawyer's writ. "I'll drop the lawsuit if the Board signs a legal document I've brought with me tonight that waives in perpetuity any and all neighborhood fees and assessments for my residence, no matter who owns it or lives in it." Unfolding it, I continued my bluff. "The Board has until I leave this meeting to sign. Once I leave, all bets are off and I'll sue the neighborhood Board."

The hum renewed, and finally Sadie called the Board members into the kitchen to confer, which didn't take long. "We'll have a lawyer look at the paper you want signed," she said.

"Nope. The wording, as you surely noted, says you sign freely with no sense of pressure or duress to do so. A lawyer will tell you my solution is an easy way out for you. If you go to court, which I'll surely win, the neighborhood will need an assessment to pay legal fees and court costs."

More conversation, this time longer, as voices rose and fell in the kitchen. Finally, they agreed and signed. I was more than surprised, shocked actually when, after Sadie announced the signing, a scattering of applause chased itself around the room. I didn't stay for refreshments either, but before I left, a couple of neighbors bumped elbows with me, said they were sorry for the treatment I'd received, were glad I'd hung tough.

Willard did later make one demand on the neighborhood, though, in order to drop his claims to the land here. He has two kids, one in junior high, another in high school. He proposed to build a home on the site of the future clubhouse and pool. He would build it to the overall dimensions of the planned clubhouse, and he and his family would live in it until the younger kid graduated from high school. Too, he would build a large patio where the pool was planned, and the neighborhood could use it for a meeting place while his family lived there. Then he would sell it to them at a price allowing him to build a small home in rural Virginia, where he and his wife planned to live out their years. If the neighborhood could agree to that, he wouldn't pursue his claim to ownership of the ridges. In fact, he would sign a paper dropping all claims to the ridges when he and his wife moved to Virginia.

Twenty-Three

Something happened in the neighborhood following the explosion I caused at that months-ago Board meeting. Neighbors began getting along, albeit somewhat superficially in far too many cases. And about Willard's proposal? Half the residents didn't like the idea at all and still oppose it. But one among them announced at a subsequent Board meeting that he would help Willard build his new home. Then three other men offered to help.

It's the Fourth of July today, and Willard and his family have been in their new home long enough to settle in, he happily exploring every shovelful of dirt, every new archaeological revelation from the neighborhood site. He personally removed the graffiti from the Viking stone and built a small, not-unattractive lean-to, sheltering it from further aging and erosion. He's published his history paper in book form, and that, added to the oddity of a Viking stone in North Carolina, means he's been interviewed by every major newspaper in the country about the dig. He synopsized Hiram's story and included it in an article about the Native American elements of his dig, and it's been published by *Smithsonian*, with multiple reprints throughout the western hemisphere. Of course, that makes him a celebrity some in the neighborhood proudly embrace. Of course, others bemoan the attention and complain constantly about it.

Around the time Willard moved into his home there, and as you might expect, I sold the house Angie and I built to a single woman — my lawyer, a situation the anti-Hardaway element of Catawba Corners despise. But not to worry; her legal reputation keeps them at bay. I rented an apartment in a new, nearby complex. I still have the mountains around me and easy access to hiking trails. My apartment neighbors, at least the ones in my building, are mostly friendly, polite, and considerate. They're not really invested in living here; they come and go, and that provides a discreet vitality you often don't find in neighborhood home ownership. Ironically, those aren't the sorts of conditions to distract me from focusing on my work, and I've managed to earn enough to pay all of Angie's hospital bills.

Why did I choose to move in the first place? It wasn't about my Board meeting stand, really, and the friction and sporadic hostility that remains over the agreement to forever waive neighborhood fees and assessments for the residents of that home. I needed a fresh start, what with Angie gone, and I couldn't manage that with her presence echoing through the house. I still pass by it on my walks, which sometimes take me through the neighborhood, to the fields beyond, and toward the mountains.

Sadly, the old divisions are returning to Catawba Corners, now that COVID has been conquered. During my walks, some of the former neighbors look up, smile, and wave, and others trot over to accost me, wanting to debate current neighborhood issues they seem compelled to blame on me. At first, I was willing to engage them, but now not so much. It's better, I think, to say hello and move on. But even from my current geographical and emotional distance, this tension between those who live there remains a palpable thing. Something that lies dormant, waiting, like a cat eying a chipmunk, to tense and pounce. Is it even possible for those there to rid themselves of this ever-evolving need for conflict, to live together in something approaching harmony? I don't know. But I do think the possibility of it, hanging out there like a carrot on a stick, is like a coin, with two sides. It holds promise of a better future, to be sure, but it's also a red flag, warning that life, in order to be better, must move on from the way things are to the way they need to be.

I've moved on in another way. I've been seeing a woman, Anna, a yoga instructor and retired literature professor from a college not far away. She's shorter, has wavy, red hair. A human dynamo, and she keeps me hopping. I don't think we'll ever marry, or even live together. Perhaps that reluctance on both our parts is a sign of the times — people's need to spend a lot of time alone in order to figure out what makes their lives meaningful, both as individuals and as parts of a social whole.

Along those lines, Angie's death has made me confront the quality of my life. When she was alive, I spent so much time worrying about whether she was happy, whether we were okay together, then keeping my clients satisfied, that I didn't take the time to look out for my own happiness. Look, I'm aware of my faults. I know I was overly protective of my right to work at home, and sometimes self-absorbed to boot. It'll be with me forever that I was responsible for Angie's death. We both had our baggage, as do most multiple-marriage folks, but we tried. God knows we tried. Creating happiness between people can be hard, though, even fleeting when you do succeed in achieving it.

It took a long time for Chris and me to repair our friendship, but lately we've been doing some tandem canoeing on the Nantahala River. Nature's beauty is forever changing, but it's always there. Seasons pass on, transferring that beauty in a way that makes it seem permanent. Like the seasons, something in me has transformed, making my work more than a livelihood. It's a way to serve others, and that's probably the most important thing I've ever come to realize.

Anna feels the same way about her yoga practice, the time she needs for the political action she's involved in locally. So we stay busy enough, living separate lives the larger part of our days and weeks. Still, we don't have to artificially make time for one another. It's spontaneous, perhaps to a fault, and our hours together go by like mere moments.

Today has been the first Independence Day since the virus tucked tail and ran, and the celebrations have been animated everywhere. Here, there's a new moon, the sky a dark velvet blue, and I can hear the fireworks my former neighbors are setting off on the patio behind the Willard home. Anna laughs and points to something far beyond the celebration's effects. I think I see it. No, I'm certain I do. As the flashes and colors illuminate the mountains surrounding us and fade to dark, I imagine them moving, just a little, like a dragon caught in her slumber, stirring and about to wake.

About The Author

Bob Mustin has had a brief naval career and a longer one as a civil engineer and has been a North Carolina Writers Network writer-in-residence at Peace College under the late Doris Betts' guiding hand. In the early 90s he was the editor of a small literary journal, *The Rural Sophisticate*, based in Georgia. His work has appeared extensively in print and electronic publications

To learn more about Bob Mustin, visit:
Website: www.bobmustin.com
Blog: bobmust.wordpress.com